HIT WITH
THE REAR

HIT WITH THE REAR

A Novel

EDMUND DOLLINGER

Full Court Press
Englewood Cliffs, New Jersey

First Edition

Copyright © 2019 by Edmund Dollinger

Published in the United States of America
by Full Court Press, 601 Palisade Avenue,
Englewood Cliffs, NJ 07632
fullcourtpress.com

ISBN 978-1-946989-25-3
Library of Congress Catalog No. 2018967634

Editing and book design by Barry Sheinkopf

To Edie

My very best friend
and the love of my later years

ACKNOWLEDGMENTS

I would like to thank my writing mentor, Barry Sheinkopf, at The Writing Center, for patiently teaching me how to turn a story idea into a completed novel. I couldn't have done it wiothout you.

Thanks also to my Wednesday night writing group classmates and critics who listened patiently to and criticized bits and pieces of this book over some years—Eugenia Koukounas, Gail Larkin, Edie Messer, Rita Kornfeld, Ora Melamed, Harold Steinbaach, Natalie Beaumont, Tony Wiersielis, and anyone else I've inadvertently left out.

Thanks as well to Fred Crabbe, Jerry Kotch, ancl Paul Lefkowitz, of the Tenafly Rotary Club, for their gracious comments.

Thanks too to Nina Altman for reading and pointing out numerous pieces of unneeded fat that I excised from the penultimate draft of this novel.

Thanks as well to my cousin, Arlene Pollack for reviewing my final draft.

Finally, I thank the excellent faculty, past and present, of the New York University School of Law for providing my hero, Bill Andrews, and his author, with an outstanding legal education.

PROLOGUE

THE CRASH WAS DEAFENING. *Joel Berger, driver of the rear car, was badly shaken—not only by the impact, but by the release of the air bag, which burst open and imprisoned him against the backrest. Before he could recover, the driver's side door was wrenched open, and a large man, his face covered by a ski mask, grabbed Berger's jaw with a gloved hand, forced his mouth open, pushed a bottle in, and holding his nose to force him to swallow, poured sickly sweet whiskey down his throat. He spilled more of the liquor on Berger, shoved the nearly empty pint bottle under the air bag, and slammed the door shut, as his victim threw up.*

Berger was still trying to free himself when he heard a siren and looked up to see a flashing light heading towards him. It must be the police. What the hell was happening?

Twenty minutes before, at 11:00 P.M., he had left a monthly gin-rummy game with his boyhood friends at his high school alumni club, picked up his car from the garage, and been slowing for a red light two blocks away when a car at the light suddenly backed up at high speed and rammed into him. The two officers from the patrol car were led to Berger's vehicle by a tall, broad-shouldered, Hispanic-looking man shouting for them to arrest the drunk who had crashed into his car, and to get an ambulance for his badly injured uncle Juan. After calling for the ambulance, the officers turned to Berger's car. The odor of whiskey and vomit disgusted them as they worked to free him from his restraints. "Let's see your license, registration, and insurance card, son," asked the older officer, who appeared younger than Berger's fifty-five.

Berger retrieved them from the glove compartment while the older officer started to question him.

The younger cop called Berger's information in and brought back a Breathalyzer.

CHAPTER ONE

I AWOKE EARLY FOR MY BRONX court date, showered, shaved, and combed my hair. My image in the mirror didn't look too bad. Straight brown hair had just traces of gray, pretty good for a forty-one-year-old. I picked a gray three-piece suit, blue shirt, and striped tie and dressed quickly. The suit hung well on my five-ten frame. I was nearly as slim as I had been when I played professional tennis. Sue beat me to the kitchen, and since the nanny had a half-day off, was getting our daughter breakfast. I kissed them both, downed a small orange juice, a few sips of coffee, and a slice of dry toast. "See you at the office," Sue called.

The adjourned conference in *Ramos v. Berger* was scheduled for 9:30 in Individual Assignment Part 32 of the

Supreme Court. I'd gotten the case after Capital Casualty took it away from Alvin Herman. The judge had apparently grabbed Herman's file, told the plaintiff's attorney there was a three-million dollar policy, and made a million-dollar offer on Herman's behalf.

I TOOK THE SUBWAY TO THE COURTHOUSE at 161st Street and the Grand Concourse, and met my associate, Alex Tietel, at the locked door of the part. Alex was the last of my second-year associates to be assigned a second seat on one of my cases. Considering what Judge Robbins had done to Herman, I'd've preferred having someone with me whom I'd worked with before, but I needed to evaluate Tietel under fire. I'd briefed him the night before.

"We're number seven, Bill," he told me.

"You ready to protect me if the judge tries to steal the file?"

"You betcha."

The door opened, and we all filed into a tiny courtroom with two rows of spectator benches. The program of turning large, dignified courtrooms into many chintzy smaller ones sucked. We checked in with the clerk, an Asian woman in her early thirties, at a desk next to the judge's robing room. "Is the other side here?" I asked.

She shook her head, pointing to a blank space on the sign-in sheet, and told us to take seats.

Ten minutes later, we checked again and saw the plaintiff's space was filled in. "Mr. Ayala?" I called out, and a short, thin man with a light-coffee complexion, waved from behind the second row of benches. His dark-blue pinstriped suit made my six-hundred dollar one appear to have come from a thrift shop.

"Bill Andrews."

"Miguel Ayala." We shook hands. "My friends call me Mike, but you can call me Miguel."

I chuckled. "We're going to get along fine. I appreciate a good stand-up comic. The guy over there is Alex Tietel."

Ayala looked Alex over. "He sure is big."

"Six-three," said Alex.

"Where's your generous friend Alvin?"

"Mr. Herman has been reassigned to the more important cases—the ones where there's money on the files."

"There's a million-dollar offer on this one."

"I wouldn't spend it if I were you. This is a no-pay case."

". . .That's not what the judge thinks."

"Then let him pay it."

The little man chuckled. "You gonna bust my balls on a simple hit-in-the-rear case?"

I nodded. "Only if they need it, and this is no simple hit-in-the-rear case. The plaintiff's driver intentionally caused the accident by backing at high speed into my client's car."

Miguel shook his head. "That's the same bullshit Alvin told the judge, who didn't buy it either."

"I couldn't care less what Judge Robbins buys.

". . . Miguel," I said quietly, "let me give you a suggestion. From what I've learned about you, you're a straight guy, and you wouldn't knowingly take a staged accident case. But when the truth comes out, someone's going to try to pin the blame on *you*. If I were you, I'd check it out now and cover my ass."

Just then the clerk announced, "Ramos against Berger."

"Moment of truth," I said, and we trooped in.

Like the rest of the part, the robing room was undersized. It barely contained the judge's scarred desk, chair, a near-empty bookshelf behind it, four metal visitor's chairs, and a clothes tree hung with the judge's suit jacket. Robbins was looking down at the file, his plump cheeks puffed out in concentration. He motioned us to seats. "Where's Alvin?"

"He's off the case, Judge. It was reassigned to me. I'm Bill Andrews, and my associate is Alex Tietel."

Robbins smiled and ran his fingers through a thick head of curly brown hair. "Needed two of you to replace him, huh. . . . Andrews? I've heard that name. Aren't you the tennis player they fired from the U. S. Attorney's office for dishonesty?"

I strained to keep the anger from my face. "Yes, Judge, and I'm also the one who got an apology and offer of reinstatement from the President of the United States, and a big chunk of money from my defamation suit against the people who spread that rumor."

The judge glowered. "Well, you'd better not do anything dishonest in *my* court. Come to think of it, do you have a license to practice law?"

"Yes, Judge. You're free to check it out."

"Don't worry, we will." Robbins looked down at the file again and turned to Ayala. "I see we're here to learn the plaintiff's response to the million-dollar offer."

I leaned forward. "Excuse me, Your Honor. My client has made no offer. There's nothing for the plaintiff to respond to."

"You don't know what you're talking about. You weren't at the last conference."

"Mr. Hermann didn't make the offer. You did. He didn't have the authority to offer anything."

"Don't you interrupt me, mister. I was there." He turned back to Ayala. "What's plaintiff's response?"

The lawyer shook his head. "A million won't do it, Judge. This is a simple hit-in-the-rear. If we can settle this now, I think we can give the insurance company a discount off their three-million policy."

The judge smiled. "That's very sensible idea. How

much of a discount do you need, Andrews?"

"There's nothing on the table, Judge. This isn't a hit-in-the-rear case. It's a staged accident. The plaintiff's car intentionally backed into the Defendant's."

"Cut the *crap!*" the judge barked. "We don't tolerate frivolous defenses in my court."

"It's not frivolous."

"Come off it. If you really have anything, let's see it." The judge reached for my file. I pulled it away.

The judge hit the intercom. "Send in the court officer."

An overweight uniformed officer in his late fifties, with a hand gun strapped to his waist, appeared

"Hand it over," Robbins demanded.

I pulled it against my body. "I will not, and if you use or threaten force, I will file criminal charges."

The judge's cheeks turned red. He pressed the intercom. "Have the reporter set up his machine."

TEN MINUTES LATER, WE WERE in the courtroom, the case was called, and I was standing before the judge. "Mr. Andrews."

"Yes, Your Honor."

"Does your firm now represent the defendant?"

"It does."

"And do I understand correctly that the defendant claims that the driver of the car in which the plaintiff was a passenger intentionally backed into defendant's automobile?"

"Yes, Your Honor."

"And do you claim that you have material in your file that backs up that contention?"

"We do."

"Mr. Andrews, I *order* you to turn your file over to me so I can examine it and evaluate your claimed material."

Holding my temper in check, I looked straight into his eyes. "Your Honor has no authority to order me to surrender my file, and I respectfully decline."

Judge Robbins beamed. "Mr. Andrews, I find you guilty of a civil contempt of court committed in my presence. I sentence you to civil jail until such time as you obey my order." He turned to the court officer. "Mr. Hanley, take this man to my chambers and keep him in custody until I sign a commitment order." He turned to me. "I trust you will enjoy your stay in the Tombs," the famous old jail in lower Manhattan that serves as the civil jail for the Bronx.

I noticed Ayala, who was watching from the plaintiff's counsel table, grit his teeth to remain expressionless.

Before I was led off, I handed the file to Alex. "You know what to do."

He nodded.

As the court officer led me out of the courtroom and into a detention room a few doors down, his rubber-soled shoes squeaked on the vinyl floors. I mulled over the situation. My steady diet of insurance defense cases bored the hell out of me. I'd never been in jail before, and the prospect was amusing.

CHAPTER TWO

JUSTICE FRANK MCKENNA, the administrative judge of Bronx County, was seated behind his desk, going over a draft of a report the chief administrative judge had asked for. Frank completed his second reading, removed his rimless glasses, and was wiping his eyes when the intercom buzzed.

"Yes, Alice."

"Judge McKenna, there's a couple of lawyers from one of the big firms. They say it's an emergency."

"Have them see Mr. Coleman," his law secretary.

"They have, Your Honor. He thinks you should speak to them."

McKenna sighed. "Okay, send them in."

"Judge McKenna," said the shorter of the two, "I'm

Mark Linstrom. I'm a partner in Franklin, Powers and Rush. This is Alex Tietel, our associate."

"Good firm," replied the judge with a nod. "What's the emergency?"

"Judge Robbins is in the process of imprisoning my partner, Bill Andrews, in the Tombs, because Bill refused to hand over his defense file so that the judge could read it out loud to the plaintiff's attorney."

The judge grimaced. "You're kidding. He has no right to your file."

"I know it, and Bill knows it, but it appears that this is one of Judge Robbins's regular practices. When the case was last on before him, he had his court officer yank the file out of the hands of the attorney then representing the defendant, and the judge told the plaintiff's counsel that there was a three-million-dollar policy."

". . .Who can verify this?" the judge asked.

"I can give you proof positive of most of it. When Bill heard what'd happened to his predecessor, he decided to cover himself by breaking a rule. He had his associate record everything surreptitiously. He can play it for you."

Judge McKenna shook his head. "You know you're not supposed to do that. . . . But let's hear it."

Alex removed a recorder the size and shape of a large pen from his breast pocket and pushed *Play*. For the next half hour they listened to a crystal clear recording of both the conference and the court hearing.

The judge pushed back a lock of curly white hair from his near-ebony-colored brow. "I think this should be handled informally. Why don't you gentlemen go out for lunch and come back in about an hour?"

"We'll do that, Your Honor. Let's go, Alex. The judge has just gotten you a lunch on the firm."

When the lawyers had departed, McKenna pressed the intercom. "Alice, please call Judge Robbins and ask him to join me—and have him keep Mr. Andrews *in this building* until after our meeting is over."

TWENTY MINUTES LATER Robbins showed up and settled himself on a visitor's chair. He was dressed in a black suit, which McKenna found amusing. "You wanted to see me, Frank?"

"Yes, Harry. Thanks for your promptness." There was no smile on McKenna's face, who leaned back in his chair and contemplated him.

". . .You're welcome," the chubby man said, breaking the uncomfortable silence. "What's up?"

"I've just heard that you've been sending big-firm partners to jail."

Robbins forced a smile. "Only one, and he deserved it."

"Oh? What'd he do?"

"Frank, are you my supervisor?"

McKenna chuckled and tapped his finger on the desk. "Among other things. I'm here to keep this court looking good—and jailing lawyers, except in extreme cases, does not enhance our image. Fill me in!"

Robbins's face reddened. "The man is a snot. He dissed me, and he refused to obey my orders."

"I assume you have a record of all that?"

Robbins's lips parted with the first hint of uncertainty. "The—the refusal to obey an order is."

"And what was the order?" McKenna laced his fingers together over his woolen vest.

"He gave me some frivolous crap about a staged accident. Said the plaintiff's driver intentionally backed into the defendant's car. He said it was substantiated in his file. When I ordered him to give me his file to inspect it, he refused."

McKenna was already shaking his head, and his eyes bored into the other's. "What right do *you* have to his *file?* The next thing you'll be inspecting his wallet or his underwear."

Robbins turned grim. "Come *on*, Frank. When I was in practice, if a judge wanted to see my file, I'd let him."

"If that ever happened, Harry, you were a damn fool. Now you listen good to me. If you sign a commitment order and send Andrews to the Tombs, his firm'll get it reversed so fast it'll make your head spin. Worse than that, the *Law Journal* article will make you, and this court, look *stupid,* and you'll be on your way back to civil court."

"You can't do that," Robbins nearly shouted. "I'll see Williams."

McKenna shook his head. "The county leader? County leaders have no sway at the appellate division, but I went to *law school* with the P.J. So I *strongly* recommend that you kill the commitment order, and, while you're at it, you tell the reporter to shred the tape. It would also be a good idea, I'd say, to recuse yourself from the case."

Robbins was grim. "Okay, I'll let Andrews off the hook—but I'm keeping the case."

McKenna shrugged. There were limits, he knew, though he ground his teeth for a moment. "Suit yourself. . . . And please send Andrews to see me after you remove his cuffs."

SHORTLY AFTER ROBBINS LEFT, McKenna decided it was time to eat. He frequently had lunch in his chambers, and this was one of those days. His wife was a good cook, and leftovers made very tasty sandwiches. He was just finishing an excellent pot roast with gravy, on Italian bread, heated in the microwave and washed down by strong black coffee, when the intercom buzzed. "Yes, Alice?"

"There are three lawyers waiting to see you, Judge."

"Is one of them Mr. Andrews?"

"Yes, Your Honor."

"Send him in, and ask the other gentlemen to wait."

As I entered, the judge rose and stuck out his hand. "Mr. Andrews, I'm Judge McKenna." He motioned me to a seat.

"Good to meet you, Your Honor."

The judge smiled warmly. "I see you're no longer wearing handcuffs."

I suppressed a chuckle. "I was fortunate in that department. The court officer didn't have a pair. He told me that my Tombs escort from the sheriff's department probably had some."

The judge scratched his head. "Do you know why you're here?"

"Not entirely. Judge Robbins said to come here, and not to run away. My colleagues told me about their meeting with you, and that you had listened to my unauthorized tape."

The judge forced a frown that evolved into an awkward grin. "Yes, using that tape is prohibited. I suggest you don't make a practice of it."

"I'll try not to, but from what I'd heard about Judge Robbins, I thought my back needed coverage."

"I understand, but save it for dire emergencies."

"Like today?"

Judge McKenna nodded. ". . .Your staged accident defense—can you prove it?"

"Not yet. The client is adamant that the plaintiff's car intentionally backed into him. The insurer has investigators on it, but from what I understand they don't have anything yet."

"Sounds like you have a tough case. Might be a good idea to settle. In my experience, the longer an unsuccessful investigation takes, the higher the settlement will be."

"You're probably right, but fortunately for me it's not my decision. I will pass on your advice." I was enjoying the meeting. This judge seemed like a good guy.

The judge crushed his sandwich wrappings into the waste basket. "Has Judge Robbins told you anything new about your contempt conviction?"

"No, he just sent me to you."

"Let me give you my prediction."

"I'd welcome it."

"He'll probably tell you that he's decided to give you a break, because it's a first offense. I suspect that you'll make a motion for him to recuse himself and want to use the record to back it up."

"Makes sense."

"I don't think you'll *find* a record of today's events to support it. I'd appreciate it if you didn't pursue the missing transcript. To do so would cause very bad publicity for the judicial system." The judge winced.

I nodded. "I understand."

"I think a motion for the judge to recuse himself, even without the reporter's minutes, is a good idea, but absent statutory grounds such as financial or family involvement, it's purely discretionary with him."

"And I assume that he won't."

The judge nodded. "I suggest you go back to Judge Robbins and allow this to play itself out. And thank your colleagues for me. They can now go about their business."

When I returned to Judge Robbins' chambers, I was kept waiting for an hour, then he lectured me, and finally pardoned me with an admonition. I returned to my office to supervise the preparation of the recusal motion.

After I left the chambers, Robbins called his law secretary into his room. "Thelma," he said to the thin Asian woman. "I have bad vibes about Andrews. Check him out."

MY LAW PARTNER AND WIFE, Sue, got home at 7:00 that evening, somewhat earlier than usual. She was smiling as she came in. She appreciated the extra bedroom, the larger living room, and full dining room we'd gotten when I sold my two-bedroom and bought the largest unit in the Ninth Street co-op. "I'm home! Who's got Marcia?" she shouted, hoping it was me rather than the nanny.

"She's with me in her room, Mrs. Andrews."

"I'll be right with you, Anna, soon as I hang up my coat." She went into the middle-sized bedroom—four-year-old Marcia's room and her soon-to-be-born sister's—where she found Anna and her slim charge working on a jigsaw puzzle. Sue ran her fingers through her daughter's curly dark-brown hair and picked her up for a hug and kiss. She wondered once again where the curls came from. Both Sue's and my hair were straight brown.

"Put me down, Mommy," the four-year-old cried. "We almost finished *picture*."

"Yes, Mrs. Andrews, she's getting very good at doing puzzles," said the full-figured blonde nanny who'd been caring for Marcia since birth.

"Good job, sweetie, only three pieces to go," Sue replied looking down at a nearly complete tiger. She turned to Anna. "Have you heard from Mr. Andrews?"

Just then they heard me open the front door. "Ladies, I'm home."

"Daddy's home, Marcia—get ready for a big kiss."

The little girl pouted. "I wanna finish *picture*."

"What picture?" I asked as I came into the room, picked up my daughter, and gave her a hug and a loud kiss.

"*Tiger* picture," she replied, squirming to get down.

I put her down and looked at the puzzle. "Hey, that's great. Good job, you're almost done. What's the next piece?"

She studied the three remaining ones with a confused look. They all contained similar-looking jungle greenery.

Studying the puzzle, I saw what she needed. "Can I give you a hint?" I asked.

She nodded.

I pointed to the tiger, which was nearly complete. "What's missing from the tiger?"

She stared intently, then her face brightened. "A ear."

"And what's this? I pointed to a piece that was mostly jungle, but with a yellow and black bit at one end.

She laughed. "*Tiger's ear.*" She picked up the piece, fitted the ear to the head, and the rest of the shape fell into place. The openings for the other two pieces were in separate parts of the jungle. She inserted them easily and looked up, beaming.

"Say thank you to Daddy," Sue told her. "He's a very smart man. He knows all about tigers."

I stifled a chuckle. Sue loves to pull my chain, and she's damned good a it.

AFTER MARCIA WAS PUT TO BED, we dined on frozen dinners Sue bought at a newly opened Whole Foods. "Marcia is doing great," I commented. "She did a super job on the puzzle."

Sue frowned. "I'm not so sure. She does puzzles alright, but her pre-school teacher, Miss. Gold, told me she's not doing well in class."

"How so?" I wrinkled my brow.

"Doesn't pay attention; scribbles instead of drawing."

I shook my head. "She'll get over it. She's only a little

girl."

Sue shook her head. "By then she won't get into a decent private school."

"Oh my God! What's this world coming to? I went to public school, and so did you."

"Things have changed. Why do you think we're working so hard?"

"I'd like to speak to Miss. Gold."

"There'll be a parent teacher meeting next Monday night. Why don't you come along?"

I entered the date in my smart phone.

After dinner we sat down in the living room, with cups of coffee, mine laced with brandy. I mused how fortunate I was having a loving wife who was also my law partner, a brilliant appellate lawyer, the mother of my daughter, and pregnant with another girl.

"Anything exciting happen in the insurance defense field today?" she asked aware of my growing boredom.

"It's a long story."

"If you tell it efficiently, we could have some time in bed before my obstetrician turns off the sex lamp."

I started to explain, and for a while Sue listened without interruption, but when Harry Robbins' name was mentioned she nearly exploded. "You've got *that* stupid bastard? You poor baby."

"You know him?"

"Only on paper. I've handled two appeals from his trials, one from civil court a year ago, and the other recently from supreme. How the man ever made a living at plaintiff's trial work, I'll never know. He doesn't know *how* to ask a question on direct that isn't leading." Leading questions were only allowed on cross-examination.

"That bad? Then he's lucky his wife's a buddy of the county leader's daughter."

"So *that's* how he got there. He doesn't have the brains to judge small-claims cases. What did he do to Jerry Arthur's nephew?" She raised her empty cup.

I went to the kitchen for refills, handed Sue one, took a sip, and continued, including my day in court.

She sipped her coffee and commiserated. "You poor baby, stuck with that ogre."

A slight smile crossed my face. "It's not so bad. Dealing with him was actually exciting. You know I've been getting bored with my run-of-the-mill insurance defense cases."

"Don't throw them away just yet. They make us a good living, and private schools for the girls will cost."

I shrugged, then scrunched up my face. "I'd like to know more about the guy, before my next conference with him."

"I may be able to help with that—but first," she rose and beckoned me with her finger.

I smiled in anticipation.

CHAPTER THREE

I EXPECTED MY FOLLOWING WEEK'S trial to have serious problems, but I got a lucky break. The research department discovered that one of the plaintiff's key technical witnesses had been convicted of perjury in a different state, under a different name. I brought it up in cross-examination and destroyed the man's credibility. Without his testimony, it would be difficult for the plaintiff to prove the *prima facie* case to get to a jury. The plaintiff's attorney scrambled to make a bare-bones case, but by the end of day on Friday it looked as though there would be a nuisance value settlement on Monday.

As I was leaving the courtroom, my cell phone vibrated. It was Sue. "Yes, M'love."

"And hello to you too, Mr. Mutt," she replied, referring to an old comic strip we both enjoyed. "What's your schedule like for Saturday lunch?"

"I'm supposed to prep my first defense witness, just in case the trial gets to it. I want to teach Ted Scott how I do it. He's in second chair, and I think he has potential. I'm sure I can be available by two, though. Where'd you want to eat?"

"I won't be there, and two's too late. Harvey says Herb Phillips has a history with Judge Robbins, and he can fill you in on him for the price of a good lunch at Monte's, but it's got to start by one."

"You're the best. I'll do some of the prep with Ted tonight. Can you get me the reservation at Monte's and fill Herb in?"

"I'll have my secretary do it. See you at home."

TED WAS A QUICK STUDY, and by 12:30 I told him to take the witness out for a good lunch on the client, then crossed Sixth Avenue under cold bright sunlight to Monte's, an upscale French restaurant opposite my office. I was looking forward to meeting Herb in person. He was a legend in the insurance defense field and my predecessor from the merged Franklin firm. He'd suffered a career-ending stroke just before the merger that got me my partnership.

I was shown to the rearmost table overlooking the Avenue, where I found Herb sipping red wine that I later learned was a sixty-eight-dollar Australian shiraz. Harvey was right, Herb was an expensive lunch. My five-foot seven-inch guest, who, even in a bright-green Master's blazer, looked like he was ready to shop funeral homes, rose slowly and extended his hand. "I want to get a look at the chap who's been using my chair."

"In person at last," I replied. "I was wondering when I'd get to meet you."

"From all I've heard, you're doing a first-rate job running the department, and you've been able to clean up Johnny Franklin's mess."

I chuckled. "Which one?" Franklin certainly made enough of them.

"His Grace's edict that I try all the cases, which kept us a mom-and-pop store. You've trained the juniors and given them cases I hear."

As we took our seats, I noticed a pleasant aroma coming from Herb's drink. "Smells lovely," I commented, pointing to the half-full glass.

"It is. Try it." Herb pushed over the bottle, and I poured, sniffed, and sipped.

". . .You're right, it's excellent."

"I only drink the best on your dime," Herb replied, raising his glass. "That goes for the food as well."

HIS TIMING WAS PERFECT—a waiter in tuxedo trousers, tie, and vest appeared, passed out menus, and announced in an effort to sound suave, "Gentlemen, our chef has several superb luncheon specials." We nodded, and he continued. "We have *soupe de pois chiches à la sauge*, a hearty chickpea and sage soup. For *les hors d'oeuvre*, there is *pissaladière*, an onion tart. For *salade* we recommend *asperges vinaigrettre*, warm asparagus dipped in vinaigrette. Our fish specialty is *loup farci à la niçoise*, bass stuffed with tomatoes and mushrooms. And we have *agneau à la niçoise*, lamb and vegetables simmered in white wine and herbs. I will leave you the menus, wine list, bar list and be back shortly."

"How's retirement going?" I asked.

"Very well once I got over the effects of the stroke."

"Have you been able to keep busy?"

"I have indeed. I've been engaged in a major project that keeps me fully engaged, and will make me an immortal in our specialty.

"Oh?" I asked, hiding my amusement.

"I'm laboring to produce, Phillips, *Law of Tort Defense.* It will be the definitive reference in our field." Herb sipped his wine and continued. "Why should the Memories of William Lloyd Prosser and John Henry Wigmore get *all* the accolades?" He referred to the authors of definitive works on the law of torts and the law of evidence.

"I look forward to reading the great work." I hoped the lie was convincing.

AN HOUR AND A HALF LATER we had dined expensively and well but made only small talk. As we sipped coffee and brandy, I got to the point. "Herb, the feast is over. It's time to pay the piper."

"How predictable. But I did promise my expertise on that great jurist, the officially honorable Harry Robbins." He picked up his snifter, inhaled, took a sip, and began. "I first met him in connection with the defense of *Ruiz v. Hoe Avenue #2 Apartment Corp.*, one of Jerry Arthur's cases. The plaintiffs were badly injured in a fall from the staircase in a rent-controlled Bronx apartment house. She was climbing up the staircase, holding an infant in her left arm, when the railing she was using separated from the staircase. She had the misfortune of being represented by Robbins.

"I have made it a practice of doing a background check on all opposing counsel." Herb took a sip of his cognac. "He started out, after law school, with Cecil Barrymore, a Bronx negligence solo."

"Like the movie Sherlock Holmes?"

"Yes, but not an Englishman. His father was Sol Bernstein. Cecil was competent in his area. He handled the small to mid-sized cases conscientiously and farmed the occasional heavy case out to the experts. His style, which Robbins adopted, was effectively bombastic. Unfortunately for our man, he didn't embrace his boss's careful attention to detail. He did, however, learn the marriage game—by courting and wedding the only child of a wealthy clothing manufacturer. His wife taught English at Taft High School and became good friends with the Bronx County Democratic leader's daughter. That contact produced significant business, and after a few years he became a partner. When Barrymore retired, Robbins inherited the practice. Had he continued his predecessor's case-selection practice and paid more attention to detail, he would have done quite well. Regrettably, his ego got in the way. He decided he was good enough to start trying the big cases. A local Hispanic lawyer referred the Ruiz case to him, and he ran headlong into me."

"Alas, poor Robbins."

Herb shrugged. "The injuries to the mother and child were substantial and, with liability and the right Bronx jury, could have produced as much as seven million. The problem was liability. It appeared that the banister separation was sudden."

"And there was a notice problem."

"Precisely. He had to prove that the landlord either had actual notice of a weak or loose railing and didn't fix it, or that the condition was there for such a long time that any reasonable landlord *would* have noticed it. Both the super and the management company testified that they'd received no actual notice, and that they inspected the property regularly. Our man had the client's family speak to their neighbors. One of them *had* noticed the loose railing the day before the accident, but he hadn't yet reported it to the super. Robbins went with that, but with no proof of how long it was loose."

Herb started to cough, and the waiter, noticing his empty water glass, refilled it. Herb took a sip, and continued. "At trial, because of the injuries and an infant plaintiff, I was able to make a near-seven-figure offer that the man sneered at. The judge allowed the case to go to the jury, which expressed its sympathy at five and three quarter million. The judge pressed Robbins to take our offer and told him he'd push us for a million, but Robbins demanded what the jury found. The judge threw up his hands and granted my motion to dismiss for lack of a *prima facie* case."

Herb motioned the waiter for a brandy refill and resumed. "Robbins immediately appealed the dismissal and Harvey Stein handled it. You might want to talk to him about it—I understand he has some goodies."

"I will," I said surprised, "but that was long before the merger of the Franklin firm into Powers & Rush. How did Harvey get involved in the first place? Was the Franklin firm farming appeals to him?"

"No way," Herb replied with a laugh. "Capital Casualty decided that we were charging too much for appeals, but my senior partner wouldn't consider any reductions, so Powers and Rush picked up the business. Ask Harvey."

I nodded.

"I have another suggestion. Call my friend Hal Goldman." Herb reached into his wallet and handed me a card.

". . .He does legal malpractice. I've heard of him. Was that involved, too?"

"In a big way. Call him. He'll fill you in—even without a lunch."

"I'll do that—and my thanks, Herb. This was a pleasure—*and* money well spent."

On leaving the restaurant, I wondered how a bright guy like that had kept from getting bored out of his mind in insurance defense, but I decided not to ask. Maybe fighting with Judge Robbins would add some zest to my dull life.

ONE EVENING A FEW DAYS LATER, at a meeting of litigation partners, I ran into Harvey Stein. "Thanks for suggesting my lunch meeting with Herb. He was a great help."

"My pleasure. He's a great guy—but an expensive lunch guest," Harvey replied with a chuckle.

"He was well worth it, and it gave me the chance to see him in person. It's not often you get to meet a legend." My mood darkened. "I hope I can see more of him, but he doesn't look too good."

Harvey shook his head. "Yeah, I heard he's going

downhill.

... Did you get everything you needed?"

"He told me a lot, but he suggested I talk to you and to a legal mal guy named Hal Goldman."

"I know Hal. I've farmed a couple of cases to him. Send my regards. ... So Herb thinks I can add to your store of knowledge?"

I nodded.

"I've got some time now. Join me for a nip, and I'll tell you what I can."

A few minutes later, I settled into a chair in the warm glow of his muted ceiling lights. Harvey removed a bottle of malt whiskey and two glasses from a tray on his credenza, got ice from a small fridge, and set the drinks before us. He seated himself, took a pull on his drink, and commenced. "You must have heard about the Ruiz case. Before that, Capital Casualty was using the Franklin firm in heavy cases for both trials and appeals. About that time, Jerry Arthur got a bee in his backside that Franklin was charging too much for appeals. He'd learned that my then-favorite associate, and your favorite wife, had developed a computer program that made appeals less expensive."

"I married a smart woman," I replied beaming.

"You sure did." Harvey nodded. "In any event, the appeal in *Ruiz* was one of three road tests to see if we could get the business."

"And you did."

"I did indeed. From what I was told, Franklin wouldn't deign to consider reducing fees. . . . The appeal went well for us. The Appellate Division affirmed unanimously, and the Court of Appeals refused to take the appeal. So the only thing of interest about *Robbins* was that he turned down an opportunity to settle. The Appellate Division was running a pre-appeal settlement program run by the law assistants. At our conference they pushed me for a million. I called Jerry, who felt generous and agreed, but Robbins turned it down flat, saying it would be immoral for him to get less than the jury had given!"

THE NEXT DAY I CALLED HAL GOLDMAN, who told me he'd be pleased to fill him in, but he was stuck at settlement conferences for the next several days. I arranged to meet him the following morning at Trial Part 14 in Supreme New York. "How will I recognize you?" I asked the man.

"Just look for the best-looking guy in the room."

It sounded like a fun meeting, and it was. I met Goldman at one of the larger courtrooms. Nearly half of its nearly hundred spectator seats were occupied. At six-foot-four, the man appeared to have been hewn from a California redwood. He told an adversary he'd be outside and led me to a bench next to the courtroom door. The hall was dimly lit, in sharp contrast to the courtroom. "Herb told me you'd be calling. He and I go back a long way—high school, college, law school."

"That's some friendship."

"Mm, and profitable, too. He's farmed a lot of cases to me. Second smartest lawyer I know." Goldman patted himself on the shoulder.

"Bet he calls you the most modest," I replied with a chuckle.

Goldman smiled. "You got it—but we'd better get started before they call me back in to make some money."

"I understand you've had some contact with Robbins."

Goldman nodded. "Beginning with a close ethics call. Some time during the trial, Herb got a call from an investigator he used. The man had been doing Buildings Department searches on a different case when he ran into a proposed inspection of the Hoe Avenue building resulting from a tenant complaint about the loose railing. Herb was afraid it might give the plaintiff his actual notice, and that it might require him to disclose it to Robbins in time for the man to make a *prima facie* case. He told the investigator to call me. I engaged the man's services. He found that the complaint was by a man named Gomez, who was in the process of returning to Puerto Rico. The investigator found the guy and got a statement from him that he'd discovered the loose railing over a week before the accident, that he'd told the super, who ignored him, and that he had then made a complaint to the Buildings Department. When the appeals in *Ruiz* were completed, my friend showed me his file. It was clear that, if Robbins had done a proper investigation, he'd have been able to recover substantial damages.

Goldman scratched his chin just above a short, square-cut beard. "I called the Ruiz plaintiffs, and they retained me to sue Robbins for legal malpractice. I sued for thirty million, in the hope of getting the seven their case was worth, or at least the five and three-quarter the jury had given Robbins. But his malpractice policy had limits of one and a half million, and while I could collect from his personal assets, an additional half million would have put him into bankruptcy. His father-in-law'd been strongly against the marriage, considering him a blow-hard boor, and had insisted on a pre-nup with all property, including the co-op, in his daughter's name. He would have allowed his son-in-law to go into bankruptcy, but the daughter pleaded with him, and in the end he loaned Robbins enough to settle for three and a half million. He insisted that his son-in-law get out of the personal injury business and loaned him enough to get a Civil Court nomination. . . . As a result, Robbins loves plaintiffs, and he *hates* insurance companies—especially Capital Casualty. He's been making himself popular with his administrative judge by settling a good number of cases. But his methods include brow-beating insurance defense lawyers into making offers beyond their authority."

I nodded knowingly. "He's upped the ante. In my case, he grabbed my predecessor's file, read the amount of coverage out loud, offered a third of the policy, and gave plaintiff's counsel three weeks to consider the offer. At my first meeting with the man, he nearly threw me into The Tombs for refusing to give him my file."

". . .How'd he get the first guy's file?"

"Court officer yanked it out of his hands. Fortunately I was ready for him."

"You've got a problem."

As I left the courthouse I wondered whether legal malpractice might suit me. It seemed an interesting way to make a living with different legal issues in each case, but where would I get the business? I shrugged and headed back to the office.

CHAPTER FOUR

L ATE FRIDAY EVENING, the dinner party was just breaking up. Concetta still had to clear the tables, put the linens into the laundry bags, and stack the dishwasher. She'd been at it since 5:30, and she was beat. Worse, the hot kitchen made her polyester blouse stick to her chest. Serving fucking white-bread parties was the pits, too much work. The pay and the tips stank, but it was what Julio wanted her to do. The information she could get for him would some day make them rich. He said their lawyer was suing the guy who'd been bragging about his three-million-dollar auto insurance.

"Move your ass, Concetta," said the manager. "I want to get home tonight."

"Okay, Mr. Spiros, I'm doing my best here." Son of a

bitch, she thought. Now he wanted her to move her ass. Earlier that evening he was grabbing it, then complaining it was too big but offering her the privilege of going to his office and sucking him off. Well, fuck him—her mouth and body were for Julio alone.

AN HOUR LATER, IN A SMALL, ONE-BEDROOM apartment on 149th Street in the Bronx, a short, heavy-set man dressed in chinos and an undershirt was seated on a recliner in a minuscule living room. He finished his beer, put the glass on a stack table, and wiped the foam from his big black mustache. "What's taking her so long?" he grumbled. She was usually home from the Friday night parties by now. He hoped nothing had happened to her. He'd hate to lose her. He didn't love her, but she filled his needs. Her salary and tips paid the rent. She was a good cook, great in the sack—and there was the information. The insurance policy had been the best so far, but he'd thought of something that could be even better. "Ole!" he shouted as he heard a key turn in the lock, and made his way to the door. "My beautiful woman is home," he said, kissing her deeply and sucking her tongue.

After she hung up her coat and scarf, he started to lead her into the bedroom, but she pulled back. "Not so fast. Let me freshen up and have a drink first. It's been a rough day."

She went to the bathroom, washed her hands and face, brushed her long, wavy dark hair, and put on lip gloss. Studying herself in the mirror, she mused on the thirty-year-old face. The cheeks could be a little thinner, but on the whole, she looked pretty good.

In the kitchen she poured herself a glass of *rioja*, cut a slice of fruit cake, and sat down at the table, where Julio was working on another beer, this one with a slice of lime. "So how was work?" he asked.

"Like always, shitty."

"Learn anything?"

"Not tonight. He kept me too busy to listen much."

". . .The customers ever use credit cards for anything?"

"For drinks. The food is paid for in advance."

"You handle the cards?"

"Sometimes, when the manager's too busy."

"I met someone who'll pay for names and card numbers. I got a little camera I'll show you how to use."

THE NEXT MORNING, THE PHONE RANG in the south Bronx apartment of Raymondo Sanchez and was picked up by a tall man with big prison shoulders and the beginnings of a gut. "*Sí?*"

"Raymondo, it's me, Julio."

"How you doing, namesake?" the man replied since both, while unrelated, were Sanchezes.

"So-so, but I'm tapped out. I could use some of my share of the three-mil case I gave you."

"No way, *hombre*, that's not the deal. When I get my piece from the lawyer, you'll get yours." He hung up. "Fucking asshole," Julio growled.

AT 9:00 THE NEXT EVENING, in a Riverdale co-op, Julie Samuels had just finished stacking her supper dishes in the dishwasher. In the bathroom, she washed up and carefully reapplied her makeup in an effort to hide the wrinkles making her thirty-eight-year-old face seem much older. She filed her right thumbnail and repaired the chipped polish. The keyboard on her office computer was hell on her nails.

She hoped he'd come soon. The gourmet bakery he had a half ownership in stayed open until eight-thirty on Fridays and Saturdays. Joel closed on Friday evenings, but the store was only a few blocks away on Riverdale Avenue, so he'd show up shortly. He was the best thing that had happened to her since her divorce from that bastard, Roger. The only good thing she'd gotten from *him* was the apartment, and her salary barely covered the maintenance.

She rose from the table and started the coffee maker. It was filled with Columbian roast, Joel's favorite, and it would go well with the unsold cake he always brought her. He was a nice, kind man and treated her like a lady, nothing like Roger. Joel wouldn't leave her with a split lip or a black-and-blue backside. He *was* a worrier, but who was perfect?

She picked up the intercom. "Yes, Frank? . . . Send him up." She put down the receiver, moved quickly through the foyer, and opened the front door just as Joel emerged from the elevator carrying the string of a pale blue pastry box in his left hand. He strode to the apartment. He wrapped his right arm around her and they kissed deeply. "Sorry I'm a little late, sweet, but there was a rush of business just before closing."

"Hey, that's what you're in business for."

"But I almost had nothing to bring. It's only a crumb cake," he replied, handing her the box.

"Anything's fine as long as I have you." She kissed him.

They repaired to the dining area behind the living room where she brought the cake, two cups, and a carafe of coffee. For the next hour they sipped, nibbled, and made inconsequential conversation, until eleven when she noticed that he was stifling a yawn. "You've got to open in the morning."

He nodded.

"Time for your beauty sleep." She rose, took his hand, and led him into the bedroom.

By eleven-thirty they were in her bed, and after an hour of comfortable sex they fell asleep wrapped in each other's arms.

At four-thirty she awakened and went to the bathroom. On returning to bed she noticed his eyes were open. "You okay?"

"I can't sleep."

She sat down on his side of the bed and cradled his head in her arms. "What's bothering you, dear?"

"That damn accident case."

"The insurance company's taking care of that, aren't they?"

"Yeah, but I'm worried. I told them it was completely phony and not to settle."

"Well?"

"What if those crooks win the case and get a huge judgment against me?"

"You have a big insurance policy."

"I have three million, but what if they hit me for a lot more? I could be bankrupt and lose everything."

"How much are they suing you for?"

"Thirty million. The insurance company sent me a notice that I was being sued for more than the policy limits and suggested I refer it to my personal attorney."

"Did you?"

"I called the lawyer for the business. He told me they always sue for big numbers, and it almost always settles for a lot less."

"You tell him that you told the insurance company not

to settle?"

He knit his brow as he tried to remember. "I don't think so."

She shook her head. "Talk to him again, and tell him everything."

He nodded. "I will. You're a smart woman, and it's good advice."

"Let me give you another piece of advice," she said, returning to her side of the bed. "Sitting up and worrying won't do you any good. It'll only depress you."

"What *should* I do?"

She motioned to him with her index finger and opened her arms.

After some tender love making Joel slept like a baby.

CHAPTER FIVE

THE LAW OFFICE OF LARRY JACOBS was in a store on Riverdale Avenue just two blocks from W&J Classic Gourmet Bakery. Twenty years before he had graduated in the top third of his Fordham Law School class. After spending the next five years at a quality mid-sized firm in Manhattan, he, and two other non-rainmaker associates, had left to form their own firm. That lasted two years, till their sweetheart sublease ran out and they were faced with a four-hundred-percent rent increase. His partners, who lived on Long Island, had moved to Queens; Larry set up shop in Riverdale, less than a mile from where he, his wife, and two children lived.

On a rainy Monday in April, not a court day, he got to his office at 8:30, half an hour before his secretary. He started the coffee maker, then checked his voice mail. Joel Berger called. He wanted an appointment as soon as possible. The man's voice was strained, and he hoped the partners weren't at a parting of the ways. Larry immediately returned the call. "Hello, Walt, Larry Jacobs. May I speak to Joel? . . . Oh, he's meeting with suppliers? He left me a message on Sunday. Please have him to call when he gets in."

At eleven, Larry was in his office. His blond-wood desk was bare except for the file he was working on. He was dictating a contract when his motherly secretary set aside her steno book and picked up the phone. "Mr. Jacobs's office. . . . Hello, Mr. Berger." She looked up questioningly at Larry, who nodded. "Yes, I'll put him on."

"Hi, Joel, how's it going? . . . You want to come over at one? Let me check my schedule." He pointed to his secretary, who looked at his appointment book, and nodded. "I'm available. What's it about. . . . Okay, you'll tell me when you get here."

"Hello, Mr. Berger. I see you're right on time." She pressed the intercom. "Mr. Jacobs, he's here. . . . You know where to go, Mr. Berger."

"Thanks, Joan." Berger passed the file room on the right and into Larry's fifteen-foot-square interior room.

Larry stacked the file he'd been working on, pushed back his curly black hair, and rose with an extended hand. "Hi, Joel."

"Thanks for seeing me on such short notice." Joel said, placing a thin folder on the lawyer's desk, and sinking into a visitor's chair.

"I always try to accommodate nice people. What's this about? It's not about Walt. . . is it?"

Joel shook his head. "No, nothing to do with the store. It's about that phony car accident case. I didn't want to say anything about in front of my partner. He'd tell me I was being an old lady."

"Anything new?"

Joel shook his head. "No, nothing new, but I'm getting worried." He had opened his folder to a letter from the insurance company.

Larry leaned forward and saw the caption with the plaintiff's name. He was about to ask his secretary to get him the file when she appeared at the door, and handed it to him. "I thought you might want it."

Larry rifled through the folder, then looked up. "What's worrying you?"

"What happens if they win big? I only have a three million-dollar policy. I know they won't get thirty million, but what happens if they get ten, or even seven? I'll lose the bakery and have nothing."

Larry raised his palm. "Slow down. Three million is a very healthy policy. I'm sure the company will be able to settle within policy limits."

Joel shook his head vigorously. "That's just it. They *can't* settle."

"Why not?"

Joel had a sheepish expression. "I told them not to. I forgot to tell you, but I told my broker that it was a phony, crooked case, and they were not to give the bums a nickel."

Larry thought for a moment. "Yeah, you should have told me about it, but I don't think it did you any harm. I'm no insurance expert, but most auto policies give the company the right to settle claims or lawsuits. I'm also sure their obligation to defend ends when they've paid out the full amount of the policy."

"You think so?" Joel asked, with a puzzled expression.

"Makes sense. If they believe the case is going against you and they can settle for less than the policy, why fight it? If the jury comes in at six or seven mil, it's going to cost them at least the three, and maybe more if a court decides they acted in bad faith by refusing to make a reasonable settlement."

Joel let out a breath. "Then I'm safe?"

"I wouldn't go that far. I think I should get in touch with the attorney who's defending you, find out what's happening, and offer your help."

"Sounds like a great idea. Thanks, Larry."

"You're welcome, but I can't charge the bakery for my time on this. It'll have to come out of your pocket."

Joel nodded.

CHAPTER SIX

THREE WEEKS LATER, I WAS SEATED at my twelve-by-six-foot mahogany desk. Just about all of my partners had curved desks. I alone preferred the straight lines of a rectangle. I smiled as I looked out at a sunny view of Sixth Avenue. I enjoyed the luxury of a Franklin, Powers and Rush equity partner's room, but wished I had something more interesting to do than routine insurance defense. I envied Sue's variety of appeals cases, but knew she deserved them.

"When are they due, Alex?" I asked my associate.

"Two-thirty. They should be here any minute," the beanpole replied, looking at his gold chronograph, that was considerably more expensive than his boss's Timex.

The intercom buzzed.

"Mr. Jacobs and his client, Mr. Berger, are at thirtieth-floor reception."

"I'll have Mr. Tietel guide them in," I said nodding to Alex.

Two minutes later the three appeared and I rose to shake hands. "Sorry to have delayed this meeting, but I just finished a trial."

"I trust you won?" said Larry Jacobs.

"I had to," I replied with a smile. "Capital Casualty doesn't like to pay for losses."

Joel and Larry chuckled.

"In any event, the broker told Capital that you wanted an update on the case, and to assess Mr. Berger's personal risk."

"That about sums it up, Mr. Andrews, but please call me Joel."

"Okay, Joel, and I'm Bill, he's Alex, and I assume you're Larry."

"That's right," the lawyer added, "and we'd also like to cooperate in Joel's defense,"

I smiled. "Fine with me. We welcome, and expect, your cooperation, but let me start by telling you where we are. The case has been assigned to a judge who doesn't like us. I've told him that you maintain that the plaintiff's driver intentionally backed up into Joel's car."

"That's what happened!" Berger nearly shouted.

"Look, Joel, *I* believe you, but the judge doesn't. He thinks that you, or maybe we, are making up a stupidly outrageous lie in an effort to defeat an open-and-shut hit-in-the-rear case."

Joel frowned. "Who cares what the judge thinks? Isn't this going to be a jury case?"

"Sure, but what do you think a jury will do after the judge poisons their minds against you?"

"Get him to recuse himself," said Larry.

"We've tried. When we asked him, he told us to make a motion, then denied it, saying he can and will be fair to both sides."

"That's bullshit—he can't and he won't," said the attorney. "Appeal the decision."

"It won't help." Unless we can show he has a family or financial connection with the plaintiff, recusal is in his absolute discretion."

"Then what do we do?" Joel asked.

"As I see it, we need a combination of three approaches. The first thing we have to do is try to find out who engineered this scam and how they did it."

"What about the plaintiff's witnesses?" Larry asked.

"We're having a hell of a time contacting, or even identifying, all of them. The police report isn't very helpful. It has a few partial names and questionable addresses. It seems that almost no one spoke English, and the cops' Spanish wasn't too good. So far our investigator hasn't been able to reach anybody. And it seems to me that the secrecy is part of the scam. The real question is why they picked on you."

Joel smiled. "That's easy. Go after the guy with the big insurance policy."

I fixed on the man. "And how did they know that you *had* a big policy?"

"Didn't one of your lawyers tell the judge?"

"Yes, but that was *after* the accident, and *after* the lawsuit," Larry said. "The real question is who knew you had a three-million-dollar policy *before* the accident?"

"Gee, I don't know—the broker?"

"Think he was in on it?" asked Alex.

I threw a him look.

"No way. Herbie's been a good friend since high school. He's part of my monthly Thursday night high school alumni group."

". . .Wasn't that where you were right before the accident?" I asked, glancing down at my pad.

Joel nodded.

"Any of *them* know about the policy?" asked Larry.

"Maybe, but they're all good friends."

I tried not to react. "We still need to talk to all of them. Get a list of their names, addresses, and phone numbers. Then Alex will coordinate with an investigator. If he's able to learn who the information was leaked to, tie it to some unsavory characters, we may be able to convince the judge he's dealing with a bunch of crooks and get us onto an even playing field."

"What happens if that doesn't work?" asked Joel.

"Then we try to settle the case within policy limits."

"That's approach two," said Alex.

I nodded.

"And what's approach three?" asked Larry.

"That's called trial practice. I go for as much discovery as Robbins lets me have, and push him as hard as I can to create reversible errors, so I can get a second trial before an even-handed judge."

"And . . . what's my personal risk?" Joel asked with a tremor in his voice.

"Too early to say, but I'll start trying to settle as soon as I learn that the search for the bad guys isn't working."

As my visitors left, I felt a warm glow. This case was giving me a chance to relieve the boredom of so many insurance defense cases. I wondered where I could get more.

CHAPTER SEVEN

CHARLIE DINAPOLI HAD RETIRED from the New York City Police Department, Detective First Grade when he was sixty. With twenty-five years on the force he had a good pension. It would have been better if he had been a lieutenant or even a sergeant, but while he was a skilled investigator, taking tests wasn't his thing. He looked forward to Florida retirement but needed to wait till his wife, Rosie, became eligible for her teacher's pension in another six years.

In the meantime he had to keep busy and make some money. His talents were very marketable, and by the time he retired, he had been hired as an investigator by Capital Casualty. Monday was his first day on the job. After completing his paperwork he was called into the office of Mark

Stevens, the company counsel. The two made an interesting contrast. Other than being male and five feet ten inches tall, they had little in common. Stevens was slim, not a muscle builder, with a full head of dark hair, while Charlie had a substantial gut, large shoulders and arms from weight lifting, and a big bald spot surrounded by wisps of white hair on top of his head.

As he entered the crowded, one-window office, the attorney rose and stuck out his hand. "Welcome aboard! Have a seat." He pointed to the only chair not loaded down with files.

"Thanks, Mr. Stevens, it's good to be here."

Mark held up a hand. "I guess I'd better give you the ground rules. Other than our president, Mr. Arthur, who sometimes likes formality, everybody in this company goes by his first name. I'm Mark."

"My pleasure, Mark. When I was on the force, my lieutenant didn't permit it. Said it interfered with discipline."

"Don't worry about that. We're going to work you hard and expect you to produce. I spoke with Lieutenant Donovan before we hired you. He says you're a first-rate investigator, and I'm here to give you your first road test."

"Suits me fine. What's it about?"

For the next half hour, Stevens filled him in on the Ramos case, gave him the file, and sent him off to see Alex Tietel.

LATE THAT AFTERNOON ALEX'S INTERCOM BUZZED. "Mr. DeNapoli is at reception."

Alex ushered him into a small conference room. "Good coffee, and china cups, too! This beats the N.Y.P.D. by a mile," said Charlie. "I'll have to visit you more often."

"The perks here are great if you don't mind the twelve-hour days that go with them," Alex replied.

"They tell me you have a list of the names, addresses, and phone numbers of the club members, including the insurance broker."

Alex nodded and handed him a copy.

"I'm going to spend the next week or so interviewing them."

"Give me your schedule, so I can arrange to tag along."

Charlie shook his head. "Mark Stevens told me not to have you along. It'll cost too much. Why don't you tell me what you want me to ask?"

"I'll put something together, but I ought to clear it with my boss first."

"How long will that take?"

"Probably only a few days."

"Get it to me as soon as you can."

FIVE MINUTES AFTER HE LEFT the meeting, Charlie was on the phone with Mark Stevens, who immediately told him, "Forget about Tietel. Just set up your meetings. I'll call Bill Andrews and have him set the kid straight."

CHAPTER EIGHT

ROCK SOLID INSURANCE, INC., was located on John Street in Manhattan, two blocks from Capital Casualty. It had been named after its founder, Saul Rockman, who'd left the business to his wife, his two sons, and his daughter, Muriel's husband, Herbert Goldstein. Rockman had, to say the least, been parsimonious. He had not wasted money on a fancy office, and the accommodations were spartan: One large general room with six desks, five of which were outfitted with a computer, a file and copier room, and a library-conference room that was better arranged to appeal to customers.

The five computer desks were occupied by the three family-member owners, a salesman who was paid strictly on commission, and Sadie, who ran the office with an iron fist encased in a steel glove. She had come on board after Saul's wife, Greta, at last decided to retire.

The sixth desk had been Rockman's until his sudden heart attack, and now sat empty as an unofficial memorial to the founder.

TUESDAY AFTERNOON AT 3:00, Herb returned to the office after beating the bushes for business. The day had gone fairly well—he'd finally closed on a second-to-die life policy that would provide him with substantial commissions for the next several years. He handed the new business to the sixty-year-old secretary, who looked like everybody's mother. "This should pay the rent for a while, Sadie." He tapped the check on the top of the stack.

"It better, or we'll be out on the street."

He picked up his phone messages and called out, "who's Charles DiNapoli?"

"An investigator from Capital. He wants to see you right away. He called three times. Says it concerns Joel Berger."

Herb immediately called the man, arranged a meeting for four-thirty that afternoon, retrieved Joel's files, and sat down in the conference room to read them while he waited for his visitor.

When Charlie got there, Herb rose to shake his hand, and motioned him to an adjoining seat at the table designed for twelve.

"Thanks for seeing me on such short notice."

"We cooperate with the companies we represent. We're on the same side, I guess."

"I'm sure we are," the investigator replied with a nod.

"I'd also guess this is about that claimed hit-in-the-rear."

"You're a good guesser.

"What can I tell you about the accident that's not in the report?"

Charlie chuckled. He was going to like this guy. "Nothing. I want you to tell me about our insured. I understand he's more than just a customer."

Herb nodded. "That's for sure. Joel and I go back a long way. We were in Clinton High together."

"Hey, that's where *I* went. When did *you* get out?" The next ten minutes were spent on reminiscence, at which point Charlie got back to business. "So tell me about Joel."

"We were part of a group of about two dozen guys who hung out together at school. It was almost like a club. After graduation, we stayed close and actually *formed* a club. We called ourselves 'De Wit's Boys.' We decided to meet once a month and have dinner, go to a show or something. It worked out better than we expected. Just about everybody who joined stayed on. As it turned out most of the guys were card players, so we held our monthly meetings at Brinks. It's a small hotel in Washington Heights that has a restaurant and catering. It's owned by the family of one of our members, so we get a good deal. We have dinner, and then the guys play cards. Joel and I were both there on the night of the accident."

Charlie nodded. "I assume that the club is a source of business."

Herb smiled. "A good one. I've sold quite a few policies there. We have two lawyers, an accountant, two dentists, a doctor, a chiropractor, a roofer, and a few other contractors. Just about everybody gets business. And Joel's a great baker, so many of us go out of our way to buy from him."

Charlie wrote this down in a notebook like the one he'd used when he was with the police department. "What's Joel like? Tell me about him."

Herb rubbed his chin. "He's a very nice guy and a good, loyal friend—but he's not too bright, and his judgment sucks. I'd trust him with my life so long as he didn't have to use his judgment."

Charlie chuckled. "How come he has a three-million-dollar auto policy? That's pretty high and, I understand tough to get."

Herb nodded. "Good question, and typical Joel. When I first sold him an auto policy it had three-hundred-thousand limits. At that time he was working for a bakery and didn't have a pot to piss in, so the three hundred was enough, and it was all he could afford."

"Three hundred thou to three mil is one hell of a jump."

"You betcha, and it was in one jump."

"Wow!" Charlie sucked on a tooth. "What happened?"

"An inheritance. He'd been working for Wally Gains-burg for a few years and doing okay but not great. Wally's a tolerable baker and knows how to run a bakery, but the quality wasn't gourmet, and the business was slipping downhill. Then he lucked into hiring Joel, who's a great baker. Shortly after he hired him, Wally realizes that he's found a gold mine. The quality of the pastry soared, business nearly doubled, and it would have grown even more with a larger store and more modern equipment. Wally was in a quandary. Investing to enlarge the business would only work if he could be sure of keeping Joel, who was only an employee and who could walk at any time. The only way to be sure of keeping him was to make him a partner, but the man had nothing to invest, and Wally was too cheap or short-sighted to make him a gift. . . . Then lightning strikes—Joel's favorite uncle dies and leaves him a substantial inheritance, which Wally talked him into using to buy into the business. Even better, Joel's investment paid for the upgrade."

Charlie nodded. "What about the three-mil policy?"

"One of Joel's defining qualities is that he's a broadcaster. The whole world has to know his business. Anything happens to him, good or bad, he has to tell everybody about it, and not just once, but again and again."

Charlie shook his head. "That's not smart."

Goldstein sighed. "Like I told you, he's not too bright, and he has no judgment. In any event, I learned about his deal with Wally when he told us about it at a meeting of De Wit's Boys. He talked so much that no one could concentrate on their cards. The next day, when I got to the office, I checked his file and realized that three hundred thousand wasn't enough coverage for a business owner."

Charlie nodded. "You were right. One serious accident, and he could lose the business."

"And end up a bankrupt working stiff."

"So you encouraged him to increase the limits."

"I called him the next day, and we made a date for lunch near the bake shop. I explained the risks, and he agreed to buy higher limits on all of his liability insurance."

"But how come three million? A million or a million and a half should have been adequate."

Herb chuckled. "That's what I tried to sell him, but as I told you, good judgment's not Joel's long suit. He panicked and demanded that I get him ten-million limits. The three million was a low-ball compromise he only agreed to because of the premium, and that was the highest coverage I could get for him anyway."

Charlie scratched his chin. "Herb, you know, I'm looking for evidence to prove that the so-called accident was a scam. The first thing we've got to find out is why they decided to pick on Joel for a car crash in such an out-of-the-way place. We all recognize that a three million dollar policy is a good reason, but how'd they know Joel had one?"

Herb nodded slowly.

"Who other than you," Charlie went on, "your co-workers and the people from my company knew the size of Joel's policy?"

"Oh, shit." Herb groaned. "Almost every member of De Wit's boys. . .but they're all our friends!"

Charlie held up his palm. "Don't jump to conclusions. I'm not accusing anybody, but learning who knew and how they found out may lead us to the bad guys."

Herb's face brightened. "How the club members found out is easy—they all heard it on the J.B.S."

"The what?"

"The Joel Broadcasting System, that's what all the guys call it."

"How does it work? He talk to one guy at a time?"

"Nah, he just shouts it out."

Charlie knit his brow. "Doesn't make sense to me. Could you give me a for instance?"

"Sure, I remember a time just a few days after I got him the three-mil policy. I had to get some paperwork out, so I was the last one to get to the meeting. Everybody was eating, and Joel was at a table next to the door. As I walked in he jumped to his feet, pointed at me, and shouted, 'Ta-ta-*tah*, presenting the world's greatest insurance agent. This guy solved my worries so I can drive in peace. He just got me a three-million-dollar auto policy.'"

Charlie took some more notes. "Jerk!"

Herb shook his head. "No, he's one of the nicest people you'll ever meet. He just doesn't have any brains."

"It could be that someone who learned about the big policy, either first hand or second hand, was able to set up the scam."

". . .Second hand?"

"Yeah, one of the members could have told someone else about it. The broadcast is a funny story. Also, who other than the club members could have heard him?"

"Well, the restaurant staff."

". . .Who would that be?"

Herb thought for a moment. "There are three or four people. They must have a cook and maybe a helper, but they'd be in the kitchen, and they probably couldn't hear anything that was said in the dining room. There's the manager, a fat guy I think his name is Spiros. He sort of hangs around, so I guess he could have heard. Then there's the waitress, Concetta, also kind of chunky. She serves the food and makes the drinks. I bet she was in the room when he shot his mouth off."

Then Charlie said, "You think I could come to the next club meeting? That way I could speak to some of the members, and I could get the lay of the land, maybe even talk to Spiros and Concetta."

"Sure. Let me talk to our president, Gary Lane. He's a lawyer, and he'll understand. Either he or I'll get back to you." A smile came to Herb's face. "We can say we're looking to expand our membership—and you *are* a Clinton grad."

CHAPTER NINE

WHEN CHARLIE SHOWED UP at the Brinks Hotel a week later, he'd already met Gary Lane, who wanted to help, and had invited him, and even thought that Herb's idea of expanding to other Clinton classes was a good one, since the club's membership was slowly dwindling.

Charlie was also getting overtime for night work.

The Brinks had been converted from a six story pre-war apartment building. Most of the rooms were let on a monthly basis or longer. There was a coffee shop on the ground floor that served breakfast to the guests and that operated as a catering facility.

Charlie had driven in order to park his car in the garage Joel had used the night of the accident. Having been told that most of the members came in their work clothes, he hadn't changed into a jacket and tie. At the front door, he was met by Herb and Gary. "Good seeing an old grad who wants to socialize with us youngsters," said Gary as he slapped Charlie on the back, tickling the investigator with his long goatee.

"I hope I can keep up with you," Charlie replied.

"Come on in," Gary said, adding in a lower voice, "I'm going to give you a general introduction as a prospective member. After dinner you can interview the others and tell each of them your real purpose as you choose." He led Charlie to a spacious dining room furnished with ten tables, five of which had been set for four. Men were having a drink at three of the tables. A heavy-set waitress was circulating among them.

They took an empty table. "This is the president's table," said Gary. "I make announcements from here." He turned his head to the entrance and motioned to Joel, who was just coming in. "Join us, there's someone I want you to meet. . . . Joel Berger, this is Charlie DiNapoli. You two have a lot to talk about." He pointed to the fourth seat at the table.

When Joel had started to ask who, Gary shushed him.

"This is very private. Keep your voice down."

The waitress came to the table for their drink orders, and handed out menus. The other three ordered alcohol but Charlie just had a soda.

"You a teetotaler?" Gary asked.

"No, but after twenty-five years on the force, I feel funny drinking on duty."

"Hey, what's this all about?" Joel asked, keeping his voice low.

"I'm a retired cop, and I work for Capital Casualty. I'm investigating that phony accident case against you."

". . .What're you doing *here*?"

"The way we see it, someone knew you had a big auto policy and set up the accident. My job is to find out who."

"How—how will being at my club meeting help you do that?"

Charlie smiled, wondering if the man was as stupid as they thought. "Good question. I understand that you told all your friends here that Herb got you a three-million-dollar auto policy? In fact you announced it at one of the meetings."

"Yeah. "So what? They're all my friends. They wouldn't do something like that."

"Probably not, but they might have told someone *else* who did—or maybe someone other than a fellow club member overheard you?

". . .Like who?"

"Like the staff."

Shortly after that, dinner was served—broiled chicken

or salmon; Charlie chose the bird, while his companions ate fish. After pie, with or without ice cream, Gary rose and clinked his glass for attention. "DeWits, I'd like to introduce my guest, Charlie DiNapoli, from the class of '88." He pointed. "Charlie's a retired police detective, and a very nice guy. I met him on a case, and when I learned he was a Clintonite, I thought we could use a few more members, and one way is to expand to other classes. I'd like to send him around to meet you, and if it turns out he wants to join, we can vote on expanding and on him."

During the games, Charlie wandered the tables, introducing himself. He asked everybody to keep what he was saying confidential, and assured them that they were not suspects but might inadvertently have passed information to someone else who could be part of a scam. He passed out business cards, and they all assured him that they'd get back to him.

He left the dining room for the open area and knocked on a closed door with a sign that read *William Spiros, Manager.* "Come in, Concetta." As Charlie entered, Spiros looked up. "You're not Concetta."

"No kidding." Charlie stuck out his hand. "I'm Charlie DiNapoli, a guest of the club and I had dinner here tonight."

Spiros's expression changed to a smile. He shook the hand and motioned him to a seat. "Good meeting you, Mr. DiNapoli. How can I help you? I hope you're not here to complain about your meal! We pride ourselves on the quality of our food and service."

Charlie smiled back. "Not at all, it was very nice. If I didn't like it, I wouldn't be here. I'm a retired cop. A bunch of us who worked together over the years formed an organization. We plan to meet a few times a year, maybe monthly. We've been looking for a small caterer for some of our meetings, and yours might be a fit."

Spiros grinned broadly. "*Great.* Let me give you a price list, some sample menus, and a copy of our standard contract." He struggled to his feet, opened the second drawer of a filing cabinet behind him, took out a folder, and laid it on the desk.

Charlie skimmed it. "Interesting. I'll show it to the guys.. ..There is one problem."

The owner's expression darkened slightly. "Oh?"

"See, all our members, being retired police officers, have picked up enemies among, you know, bad guys who might be looking to do them harm. So the staff's got to be squeaky clean."

"Have no fear. We do a background check on all our employees."

Charlie nodded. "I'm sure you do, but we like to do our own. So if you give me a list of the names, addresses, phone numbers, and social security numbers of everyone who works here, we can check them out, and if they're all

clean—as I'm sure they will be, we can sign up and start setting up dates."

Hungry for new business, Spiros complied.

CHAPTER TEN

THE FOLLOWING DAY, CHARLIE CALLED one of his friends on the force and asked him to run a record search on the caterer's five employees. The cook, it turned out, had an assistant and a dishwasher. He called Mark Stevens, who told him to drop by.

"Going to the meeting was a great idea—overtime well spent," Mark said. "What'd your buddy from the force come up with?"

"Something, but less than I'd like. Concetta, the dumpy waitress, is my best suspect. She must have heard his speech about the three mil. The phone number she gave her boss is listed under Julio Sanchez, and my friend ran his rap sheet, too."

Stevens nodded. "What did it show?"

"She has three arrests for soliciting but no convictions."

"Sounds like no buyers," Mark chuckled. "What about him?"

"Sanchez has three convictions, one low level drug, one for petty larceny, and one for fraud."

"An interesting team," Stevens commented with a nod. "What about the witnesses on the police report?"

"That's where things get dicey." Charlie flipped to a page in the main file. "The police report shows two Sanchezes, neither with Julio's address. Your claims man tried to interview them both but couldn't find either. Neither was living at the address on the police report." Charlie grimaced. "In fact, none of the three witnesses can be located."

"When are you going to interview the waitress?"

"I don't think I should. Have one of your other investigators do it. I don't want to blow my cover with the caterer."

Mark nodded. "What about the car the plaintiff was in? Who owns it?"

"Your claims man checked that out. It was owned by a used car lot that took it in trade. They claim a salesman loaned it to a friend who brought it back wrecked. They fired the guy— who also can't be found."

"Sounds fishy. Tell you what, ask Alex Tietel what the attorneys got in discovery."

A FEW DAYS LATER, DICK WILSON, Capital's original investigator, filed a report. He had tried to interview Concetta, but she refused to speak to him. The only thing she told him was she had no recollection of hearing about a big insurance policy, and that she minded her own business and didn't listen to customers' conversations.

Early one evening Alex caught me in my office, seated at my desk, jacket off, collar open, my red-and-blue polkadotted tie hanging loose. "What's up?" I said.

"On Ramos, we need the names and addresses of the plaintiff's witnesses."

I looked at him and wondered how I'd gotten stuck with this dummy. "What's their response to our discovery demands? We did *ask* for witnesses—didn't we?"

"Of course. The only response was 'see attached police report'."

"So?"

"All the addresses are wrong."

I strained to keep my voice even—the kid was not sharp. "So what are you going to do?

". . .Make a motion."

"To do what?"

"Compel discovery." The man's churning stomach showed in his voice.

"Is there anything you'd do *before* making the motion?"

Tietel's confusion was plastered on his face. "Like

what?"

"Don't you want to do something with Mr. Ayala?" I asked, not letting him off the hook.

"The plaintiff's lawyer?"

I nodded and, because Alex looked terrified, I felt sorry for him and continued in a more soothing tone. "Look—go out, get yourself a cup of coffee, think about it, and see me in an hour."

The man fled, and an hour later was back with a smile on his face.

"Got the answer?"

"I've got to write him a letter explaining, in detail, exactly why the response didn't comply with the demand."

"Why?"

"Either I get the information I need, or, if he doesn't respond properly, I make myself look better in the motion, since I'll attach a copy of my letter to it."

"Right," I said nodding approvingly. "Now write the letter, but let me see it before it goes out."

"My letter?"

"Sure—you're a lawyer, aren't you?" I grimaced inwardly. Being Alex's kindergarten teacher didn't appeal to me, but at least it wasn't routine.

AS WE EXPECTED, THERE WAS NO RESPONSE to the letter. On my instructions Alex followed up with phone calls to the plaintiff's attorney, and when Ayala finally deigned to speak, the man told him he didn't do defendant investigations. Alex prepared the motion for discovery, detailing their efforts and the other side's refusal to cooperate. The answering papers repeated that they weren't required to do the defendant's work.

On Wednesday, the return day of the motion, Alex was in court to submit his reply papers, together with a memorandum of law showing that the plaintiff's attorney was refusing to furnish discovery. As he rose to submit, the judge asked, "Where's the crooked tennis player?"

"I beg your pardon, Your Honor?"

The judge glared at him. He was reading the report Thelma had given him about me—my Columbia magna, N.Y.U. law review—just like his fucking brother, Cal, daddy's favorite.

"You heard me. Where is he?

"If Your Honor is referring to Mr. Andrews, he's on trial in the Eastern District."

"Does that man think he's too good to appear before me?"

Alex was flustered. "But, Your Honor, this is a discovery motion. The rules don't permit argument."

"Don't tell me the law, sonny. I'll see counsel in my robing room at the end of motions."

For the next hour Alex listened to eight pairs of lawyers

argue motions and was relieved to find he wasn't the only one subjected to the judge's abuse. After the final argument, the judge retired to his robing room, and Alex went up to the clerk. She looked at him sympathetically. "He has several conferences. I'll call you when he's ready."

Forty-five minutes later, except for Alex, Ayala, the reporter, and the clerk, the courtroom was empty. Her phone buzzed, and she motioned to the two lawyers. "The judge has an important luncheon meeting. Come back at two."

WHEN THEY RETURNED, the room was being set up for the continuation of a jury trial. They approached the clerk who told them to wait. The judge would get to them. It was a breach-of-contract-case, and for the next hour and a half they listened to the direct testimony and cross-examination of two of the plaintiff's witnesses. Another half hour went by.

When the clerk's phone finally buzzed, she sent Alex and Ayala in.

They found the judge seated over a file at his desk. Keeping his eyes focused on the file, the judge motioned them to seats.

Ten minutes later, he raised his head and studied his visitors. "Where the hell is he?" On hearing no response, he pointed at Alex. "The crooked tennis player. I distinctly remember ordering you to get him. Isn't that right, counselor?" he concluded looking at Ayala.

"Yes, Judge."

"Your Honor, Mr. Andrews is presently trying a case before Judge Leonard in the United States District Court for the Eastern District of New York. Besides, the discovery motion before Your Honor was made by me, not Mr. Andrews."

Judge Robbins stared daggers at him, then turned to Ayala. "Are you available this Friday morning?"

The lawyer took a diary out of his breast pocket. "Yes, Judge."

The judge pressed the intercom and told his clerk to send the reporter in with the *Ramos* file. The slim, gray-haired man entered the robing room, set up his machine, hit several keys, and nodded.

"It is ordered that the motion by the Defendant for discovery before me is hereby adjourned to Friday, May 3, at 9:00 A.M. William Andrews is directed to be present at that time."

When he left the courthouse, Ayala made a call. "Hi, Maria. Let me talk to Mr. Ortiz. . . . Hello Carlos. . . . Yes the case is moving along, and the judge is being very helpful . . . . Yes. There's a *big* problem, the witnesses. You need to give me the witnesses. I need them *now*. . . . No, I can't be patient. The judge will have to order me to give their names and addresses, and the defense lawyers will want to examine them. . . . Yes, I know they're family, but I can't wait too much longer."

AT 10:30 THE NEXT MORNING, Justice Frank McKenna was presiding over the trial of an interesting non-jury case. The direct testimony of one of the plaintiff's officers had just finished, and the defendant's counsel had risen to cross-examine when the clerk signaled McKenna. He held up his hand to stop the attorney and announced: "Off the record." Then he motioned the clerk up to the bench. "What's up, Paul?"

"Judge Leonard from the eastern district is on the line."

"Hi, Bob, how are you? . . . Great. How's Estelle? . . . Cora and I really enjoyed our weekend in Barbados. . . . And to what do I owe the pleasure of this call? . . . He did *what*? . . . No, don't call him. I'll take care of it." He turned to his clerk. "Call Judge Robbins' chambers and tell him I must see him in my chambers at one."

THAT AFTERNOON ALEX RECEIVED A CALL from Judge Robbins' law secretary informing him that the Friday meeting was off and that the motion would be marked submitted.

Two weeks later a decision came down denying the motion, sanctioning the defendant's attorneys $10,000.00 for making a frivolous motion, and providing that the defendant's attorneys pay the plaintiff's attorney the reasonable cost of his legal services in defending the motion. When I read the decision, I called Mark Stevens to cover my ass. Thank God, he sounded sympathetic.

CHAPTER ELEVEN

THE MORNING AFTER I READ the decision, I was seated at the messy desk of my partner, Gordon Jones, head of the litigation department. Gordon was the same short, barrel-chested guy I'd met ten years ago, when I was a law school senior, except that he'd lost most of his hair and the remaining fringes were snow white. After a little small talk, Gordon asked: "What's the problem?"

I filled him in on the war with Judge Robbins.

"You really know how to pick them," Jones commented after finishing the cold dregs of his third post breakfast coffee.

I nodded.

"I think you ought to get rid of him."

"But how?"

"You might try the Jonathan Franklin method," Gordon replied Franklin, once head of the firm, had contracted to have me murdered.

"You know how that one worked out," I replied dryly— Franklin had been killed in prison to keep him from implicating his murder broker.

Jones chuckled. "Why don't you speak with Judge McKenna? He seems to have a way of keeping Robbins in check—but that's no substitute for an appeal."

"You're right. I'll ask Sue to handle it as soon as she recovers from increasing the size of the Andrews family. And thanks for the suggestion about McKenna. I'll make a date to see him." I was getting a kick out of the Robbins opera. I'd been tempted to ask Gordon for some non-tort cases, but I was sure my current practice was too profitable for the firm to make any changes.

As soon as I got back to my office I left a message for McKenna. The return call came during the lunch hour. When I asked for an appointment, the judge asked whether it concerned Judge Robbins, and when I said it did, asked me to meet him in his chambers at 5:30 that afternoon, and "maybe we can talk about it."

The waiting room was empty when I got there, so I knocked at the closed door to the judge's private room and he called out, "Come in, Mr. Andrews."

The judge, behind his desk, was in shirt sleeves, drinking coffee from his *Your Honor mug*. "Care for some?" he asked, pointing to a drip coffee maker on the credenza behind him.

It smelled good. "I'd love some. I almost never turn down coffee."

"I only have powdered creamer," said the judge, pointing.

"No problem. I drink it black with no sugar, as nature intended."

"A man after my own heart." McKenna poured some into a container for me, and motioned me to sit. We sipped in silence for a few minutes. Then the judge spoke. "Before I can decide whether we have this conversation, I have to set a few ground rules."

I nodded.

"Anything I tell you is in strict confidence, and you may not reveal it to anyone without my prior consent."

"I agree. You have to protect the system."

"And no recording."

I removed the pen-sized recorder, I'd used at my first Robbins meeting, from my pocket and laid it in front of the judge. "It's off."

"Okay, I believe you're an honest man and I can trust you. I know what Robbins has been doing to you. Bob

Leonard and I go back a long way. We were in the same law school fraternity together, and our wives are good friends. He called me when you told him about Robbins' stupid order adjourning the federal trial. I called Robbins in and persuaded him that he doesn't run the federal courts. And I was told he allowed your motion to be submitted. That about it?"

I shook my head, reached into my case, and handed McKenna a copy of the Robbins decision.

"Oh, my *God*!" said the judge after he finished reading. "What did your motion ask for?"

"The names and addresses of all witnesses to the accident. The police report has every address wrong, and we can't find any the people."

The judge knit his brow. "That's routine. We give that every day. You'll win the appeal with no problem. How can I help you?"

"How do I get *rid* of him, and get someone even handed?"

The judge half chuckled. "Good question. I wish I had the answer. I'd love to kick him back down to civil court and have them replace him with someone who has a judicial temperament. I have a friend in the appellate division who could probably do it. I spoke to him the other day—but he's afraid to touch it."

"Why?"

"Judge Robbins was smart enough to marry the right woman. His wife is the best friend of the Democratic county leader's daughter. He'd have to do something profoundly outrageous in order to get bounced."

"What about a huge number of appellate reversals? . . . Nah, that would take years."

The judge thought for a while, scratching his chin. "Only thing I can think of is catching him in something that will result in bad publicity, but *that* will probably cause a worse public image for the court, and part of my job is to prevent that."

"I guess what we need is a compromise, something that looks worse for him than for the system."

"Any specifics you can think of?"

"One thing that affects me, you mean?"

"Such as?"

"He's been referring to me as 'the crooked tennis player' in open court."

"That was from the big-firm partner who tried to have you murdered and then got himself killed at Rikers?"

"Yeah! He got mad at me when I stopped giving tennis clinics for his clients, spread the word that I was incompetent and dishonest, and eventually got me fired from the U.S. attorney's office."

"And you got a full apology from the government. I guess Robbins only reads what he wants to read. What do you think you can do with it?"

"I know he said it when my associate answered the motion calendar. I'd like to order the transcript and, if the remark is there, give it to a newspaper."

"It *might* start a fire and give the appellate division an excuse to ship him back, but what makes you think it'll be *in* the transcript? I think Robbins is cute enough to lean on the reporter to leave it out."

"I *don't* think it will be in there. In fact, I hope it won't be."

"How's that?"

"If it's *not* in there, I have my associate make a motion to re-argue the motion. He'll be there on the call of the calendar ready to argue. I'll bet the judge asks for the crooked tennis player again, and that the words won't be in the transcript.

"And?"

"Say there happens to be a reporter in the courtroom."

McKenna smiled. "Ah! So you're a *devious* honest man . . . . Order the transcript, show it to me, and I'll think about it."

As I left chambers, I was pleased that there were some wise judges like McKenna who were credits to the system.

CHAPTER TWELVE

THE NEXT MORNING, I TOLD Gordon Jones what the judge had said. "Looks like we did the right thing," Jones replied, mopping spilled coffee from a file he'd been working on.

"Of course, I won't call in the press until I get the judge's blessing."

"You're right there, but you'll need a reporter you can trust. . . . Know one?"

I shook my head.

"Try Hal Roberts from the *Post*. . . . But before you talk to him, run his name by McKenna. He's been around for a long time, has good instincts, and he probably knows Hal better than I do. He may also have a better choice."

I summoned Alex Tietel to my office and brought him up to speed, then told him to prepare the motion for re-argument and give me a draft by the next day.

The next afternoon I found the draft of the motion on my desk with a memorandum of law. As I was beginning to expect, it was excellent. The young man had been the research editor of the *Yale Law Journal* and wrote well. If he could only overcome his insecurities, he'd have a future in the firm. I made a few notations, and called him in. Alex entered hesitantly, his head down. He brightened when he saw me smiling.

"Great job. It's just what I wanted. I made a few minor changes. Get it into final form, serve, and file it."

"Sure thing."

"Oh, and one other thing—order the minutes when the original motion was on."

"When the judge said all those nice things about you?"

I nodded.

Alex was about to leave but hesitated. "What do I say if they ask what I want it for?"

"Tell them your boss wants it."

THE NEXT WEEK, I FOUND a three-page transcript of the motion calendar on his desk. Attached was a yellow Post-it with a note from Alex: *I don't get it.* I examined the transcript. It contained colloquy from several of the motions, but on *Ramos* the only notation was: *submitted*. There was no mention of "crooked tennis player."

I called Alex and asked, "What don't you get?"

The young man replied: "What happened to everything the judge and I said?"

"What do you think happened?"

"The reporter is supposed to take everything down."

I nodded. "I think he probably did."

"Then why isn't it in the transcript? . . . You think the judge told him to leave it out?"

I smiled with my next nod. "It's just what I expected. When's the motion on the calendar?"

"Two weeks from Wednesday."

"Good. You may have an observer in court."

When Alex left, I called Judge McKenna, and at 5:30 that afternoon was seated at his desk, again drinking coffee with His Honor. "Bring me up to date," McKenna said.

I handed him a copy of the motion transcript. "That's the reporter's minutes for the motion calendar where Judge Robbins told my associate to get the 'crooked tennis player'."

The judge nodded when he finished. "I see everybody else's colloquy is included. What do you want to do?"

"I'd like to have a responsible reporter in court when my associate answers the calendar for the motion to reargue. My partner, Gordon Jones, also suggested I speak to

Hal Roberts from the *Post*."

The judge sipped coffee. "Good choice. If I bless your plan, Roberts is the one. When's the motion on for?"

"Two weeks from this Wednesday."

"Okay, let me mull on it for a few days. I'll probably speak to my friend in the appellate division. . . . I wonder if Robbins is stupid enough to pull that stunt again."

A FEW DAYS LATER, I HAD ANOTHER meeting with Judge McKenna. The judge looked somber. "Look, I . . . May I call you Bill?"

"Of course, Your Honor."

"I can't sanction the newspapers. My friend at the appellate division kaboshed it. Said the powers that be would have a fit. He suggested there be a neutral observer who will make an affidavit of what Robbins says to your associate."

I frowned. "Who could that be?"

"I wish I knew," the judge replied, somberly. "I'm getting a new intern from Fordham Law School who Robbins won't recognize. I thought I'd send her in to listen to the motion calendar and write an affidavit, but my friend absolutely forbade it. He doesn't want me involved. He has something in mind but wouldn't fill me in. So all I can do is wish you good luck."

"Thanks for your efforts, Judge," I said as I left.

I reported the judge's response to Jones, who commiserated with me, and I decided to use the man's sympathy as a wedge and commented: "Mark told me about the Atkins case. It sounds fascinating."

Gordon's face lit up. "It sure is; great issues of libel and constitutional law, and a defendant with deep pockets. . . . But please don't ask me to include you. I know you're bored with non-Robbins insurance defense, but you're too profitable to the firm to dilute your specialty,"

"Oh, well," I replied with a shrug. "I tried."

Gordon smiled wistfully.

EARLY THAT WARM SUMMER WEDNESDAY, Alex trudged up the long, wide staircase to the entrance of the Bronx County courthouse, his stomach in knots. He arrived at I.A.S. Part 32 about ten minutes early. The calendar, tacked up on the bulletin board, showed he was number eleven of twenty motions.

The door opened, and the room gradually filled up. He reread the motion papers for the umpteenth time. When he was half-way through he felt a tap on his shoulder. "Hey, big masochist, ready for another whipping?"

He looked up at the smiling face of the plaintiff's lawyer. The man was dressed in a well-cut, brown-checked summer suit. "No, it's your turn today, Miguel."

"Only my friends can call me Miguel. . . . Of course, if

you'll pay me the $4,500.00 you owe me, I'll make you my temporary friend."

"What $4,500.00?"

"That's what the judge gave me on your last frivolous motion." He handed Alex a copy of an order, and pointed to where Alex was to acknowledge service.

A few minutes later, the clerk announced, "All rise," and the Honorable Harry Robbins entered his courtroom, took his seat on the bench, and instructed the clerk to call the calendar. Most of the first ten went peacefully, although there was a little nasty colloquy between the judge and one of the attorneys on number five. When number eleven was called, Alex answered, "For the motion," and Ayala responded with, "Ready opposition."

"Well, look who's here," said the judge with a smirk. "Where's the crooked tennis player?"

Alex gritted his teeth as his stomach began to turn sour. "Is Your Honor referring to my boss, Mr. Andrews?"

"Of course I am. What are you, stupid?"

"Mr. Andrews is selecting a jury in Supreme Kings."

"The man's still avoiding me. Does he think he's too important to come to my court?"

"No, Your Honor, but this is *my* motion."

The judge looked down at the file for a moment. "Mr. Ayala, has this man paid you the fee I ordered?"

"Not yet, Your Honor," he replied smiling.

The judge's face reddened. "How *dare* you come into my court and intentionally disobey my orders."

"I didn't disobey your order, Your Honor. I-I was only served with it five minutes ago."

"Well, get busy with it. You can write the check now."

Alex shuddered. "I-I'm not authorized to sign firm checks."

"Why not? It's only petty cash to a big firm like yours. I was very kind to you—the fee should have been much higher."

"But—"

"Go back to your office now and get this poor man's check." The judge turned to the clerk. "Call the next case."

"B-But, Your Honor, I have a motion on."

The judge scowled at Alex. "Denied. . . . No, I'll read it, it's probably frivolous. Now get this man his money."

When Alex filled me in, I regretted the absence of a neutral observer. I thought Judge McKenna's friend was wrong, but perhaps *I* should have hired someone—maybe next time.

CHAPTER THIRTEEN

HE TRANSCRIPT OF THE MOTION CALENDAR, though it reported the colloquy for other motions, showed only that mine had been submitted. I also received a decision denying the motion, declaring a penalty for a frivolous motion, and directing the defendant to pay the plaintiff's legal expense in defending it. I furnished copies to Judge McKenna together with Alex's memo of what happened. The judge called me. "Bill, I read what you sent me. The man's a horror. I wish I could help, but my friend downtown told me the word was to keep hands off."

"I understand, Judge. Thanks for your efforts."

I realized that my only option was to appeal the bad decisions and get whatever discovery was available to me in the meantime. I called Harvey Stein to assign the best appeals lawyers he had available. I would have preferred to have Sue handle it. She's the best, but her delivery date was imminent. Harvey assigned his partner, Gary Edwards, so I knew I was in good hands.

I had Alex prepare and send out deposition notices for the plaintiff, and for all of the witnesses named in the police report, and subpoenas directed to the latter, and sent them out to a process server to attempt service at the addresses shown.

A week later, Ayala noticed the deposition of the defendant, and served a motion for a protective order, preventing, or at least delaying the plaintiff's deposition. The motion stated that the plaintiff was in a nursing home, attempting to recover from his injuries; that his health wouldn't allow him to be deposed at that time; and that his deposition would serve no useful purpose. The motion was supported by several affidavits—one from a physician stating that to appear at a deposition would be injurious to plaintiff's health and physical condition. Another was by the plaintiff, in Spanish with a translation, giving the date of the accident, that he had been a passenger in the front seat of his nephew's car; that he had felt a strong jolt behind him that drove his face into the windshield; and that he had woken up several days later in the hospital.

THAT EVENING, JUDGE HARRY ROBBINS returned from court to his Riverdale co-op. In the kitchen he noticed that the light on the answering machine was blinking. There were two messages, both from Myrah, the first telling him she was stuck at a staff meeting in school, and the second that she'd had coffee with Kathy, was on her way home, and would pick up dinner. A few moments later his wife, a woman in her forties with dark curly hair and plump cheeks similar to her husband's, came into the kitchen. She laid a paper bag on the counter and gave Harry a peck on the lips.

"Smells good. What is it?"

"Your favorite, Hungarian chicken stew. Greta made a batch today. Now let's sit down and eat before it gets cold."

He grabbed an open bottle of California chardonnay from the refrigerator, poured two glasses, and set them on the small round table in the dining alcove, while Myrah ladled stew onto plates. After dinner he made coffee while she did the dishes.

"How'd the meeting go?" he asked. "Anything earth-shaking?"

"No. Same old nonsense. My principal thinks he's supposed to hold one every two weeks, so he goes through the motions."

"How's Kathy? Have a good coffee klatch?"

Myrah frowned. "She's fine, but the meeting wasn't really social."

". . .Oh?"

"She wanted me to pass on a warning to you."

"Warning? About what?"

"It's from her father."

"The Honorable Gareth Williams?" he asked with a cackle.

She shook her head. "It's not funny, Harry. He says you've been embarrassing him."

Robbins's brow knitted. "I don't understand. . .what does he say I've done?"

"It's about a case before you, an automobile accident. He says you're giving the defendant's attorney a very hard time, and it's giving the court system a bad name. They want to send you back to the civil court. He's been protecting you, but they claim he's interfering with the judicial system."

His face reddened. "Oh, my *God*, he's in their pocket. He promised not to interfere with my cases. It's Capital, the insurance company that screwed me. They must be putting in a fix. It's a heavy case, absolute liability, and a big policy—a hit in the rear—and they're putting in a bullshit defense that the plaintiff backed up into them. Ever hear of something that stupid?"

"Mr. Williams says you're not letting them put in their defense."

"Of *course* not, it's *frivolous*. I'm doing them a big

favor, letting them make a reasonable settlement with a discount from the policy limits. If this goes to a jury, they'll get killed, and the chances are they'll have to pay more than the policy because they refuse to make a reasonable settlement in an open and shut case. I'm just beating them up a little to open their eyes . . . and now they're putting a *fix* against me? Well, I'll fix *them*."

Her stomach turned sour. Why does he keep doing this to himself? she wondered—and to *me*.

CHAPTER FOURTEEN

THE DEATH OF HERBERT PHILLIPS came as a shock to the lawyers and staff of Franklin Powers and Rush. We'd known he was ailing, and was about to retire at the time the Franklin firm merged with Powers & Rush. His first minor stroke had given me the opportunity to try one of the cases that solidified my partnership and helped to retain Capital Casualty for the merged firm. He didn't look well at our first meeting, but no one had expected the major stroke that finally did him in.

I got advance notice early one afternoon after settling a case in Brooklyn federal court. Among my messages was one from Hal Goldman. "Hi, Hal, how's it going?"

"I'm fine, but . . . Herb is in a bad way. He had a massive stroke, and he's in a coma."

"I'm sorry to hear that. What's the prognosis?"

"Not good. Nora plans to have the plug pulled tomorrow."

"Nora?"

"His wife. She wants to talk to you."

"What about?"

"She wants you to give one of the eulogies at the funeral."

"Me? I didn't know him that well. I only met him in person once about Judge Robbins. That was when I met you."

"I know, but Herb's a strange duck. He's been planning his funeral for years. He added you after the meeting. You're his successor as the world's greatest insurance defense lawyer."

"Then how can I say no?"

"He's in neurology intensive care at New York Presbyterian. Nora asked if you can come over *now*?"

I let out a breath. "I'm on my way."

A taxi ride later, I found myself in a small, sparsely furnished area that served as the waiting room of the intensive care unit. Hal Goldman, and a slim, dark-haired woman in her fifties, nearly six-foot tall, rose when they saw me.

"Nora, this is Bill Andrews, Herb's successor at the firm."

She stuck out her hand. "Mr. Andrews, thanks for your

prompt response. I know it's an imposition."

"Not at all, Mrs. Phillips," I lied, "and please call me Bill."

"And I'm Nora," she said.

"I'm going to get some coffee," said Hal. "Can I get you some?"

"Yes, please," replied Nora. "You know how I like it."

I shook my head, and Hal departed. "I understand Herb's not doing well," I said.

"He's brain dead. I have his health proxy, and I'll have the respirator turned off tomorrow."

"I'm terribly sorry."

"Thank you." A tear ran down her cheek.

"I'm a little confused about being asked to give a eulogy. I didn't know him that well, and I'm not sure what to say."

She smiled and patted my hand. "Don't worry, you'll be one of thirty-one. . . . Besides, Herb's a very thorough man. He wrote yours the week after you met. Hal will email it to you."

HERB DIED THAT FRIDAY, and the funeral was held on Sunday. There was a huge turnout. Nearly everyone from the firm attended along with many members of the defense bar and representatives of the casualty insurance industry. The main eulogies were given by Nora, her two sons, and Hal Goldman. The other twenty-seven, all written by Herb, were delivered by lawyers and insurance people including Jerry Arthur, Mark Stevens, Gordon Jones, and me.

After the funeral and grave side service, many attendees, including Sue and, me went to the Philipses' Scarsdale home.

Later, at home, Sue and I had coffee before going to bed. "What was that meeting about?" she asked.

"What meeting?"

She frowned. "You know what meeting, so stop stalling. The one with Nora, Hal Goldman, and Gordon."

I shook my head. "It was nothing much."

Her frown deepened. "Bullshit! If it was nothing much, why have you been in a blue funk ever since?"

As usual she read me perfectly, but I tried to wiggle. "I'm still mulling it over, so I'm not ready to talk about it yet. Besides, I know what you'll advise me to do."

"Come on, out with it."

"Okay. They told me he was working on a set of books since he retired. It was going to be the ultimate insurance defense bible. I knew about it, because he mentioned it at our Robbins meeting. He thought it would make him another William Prosser."

"Sounds like a great idea. It's a shame he died before he finished it."

"He'd put a lot of work into it. There's a detailed outline and drafts of much of the material. It's probably ready to submit to a publisher for a contract with a big advance, but. . . . Herb left a slew of post-mortem demands with Nora and Hal, including that I finish it and become his co-author."

Her face lit up. "That's, *terrific—Phillips and Andrews: Defense of Tort Actions*. It will make you rich and famous and be great marketing for the firm."

My face hit bottom. "That's what I thought you'd say, and it's true."

"But?"

"Insurance law is a recipe practice, and it bores the hell out of me. Now you want to make me rich and famous by writing the damn cookbook."

I tried to resist, but a week later, recognizing I had no choice, I got two copies of what Herb had produced, gave one to Alex, and took one home for bedtime reading.

CHAPTER
FIFTEEN

T HAT WAS A GREAT MOVIE," JULIE SAID, unlocking the apartment door. "I never laughed so much."

". . .Yeah, it was okay."

She considered his hangdog expression as he hung their coats in the hall closet. "What's bugging you, tonight?"

"Nothing."

"Joel, you're an open book." She took his hand, led him into the living room, pushed him down on the couch, and sat down next to him. "Come to mama."

He climbed into her open arms and nuzzled. She let him absorb her body heat for a while. "What is it?"

"It's not fair to keep bothering you with my insecurities."

She shook her head. "The hell it's not. In case you didn't know it, I love you. I'm here for you, just as you've always been for me."

He smiled. "I love you, too. It's still that damn case. The lawyer wants me for my deposition."

"So?"

"I've never *done* a deposition before."

"You'll *learn*. Stop worrying. From what you've told me, you have a very good lawyer. He'll prep you before, and you'll do so good that they'll nominate you for an Oscar. Now come with me, and I'll make you feel better."

WEDNESDAY MORNING, JOEL FOUND HIMSELF in a small conference room in the Rockefeller Center offices of Franklin, Powers and Rush. Alex and I sat next to him. I had ordered coffee and cookies, and, knowing that my client was tense, engaged in small talk as we drank and nibbled until I felt Joel had loosened up. Then I got into the case. "Now, let me brief you on what's going to happen today. In about an hour and a half, the plaintiff's lawyer, Miguel Ayala, and a court reporter, will be here to take your deposition. It was originally scheduled for his office, but his conference room is jammed—and besides, I serve better coffee and cookies."

Joel chuckled. "The cookies aren't bad, but I bake better ones."

"I'll keep that in mind," I replied. "Mr. Ayala is going to ask you questions about the accident and probably about what happened before."

I handed Joel several sheets of paper. "This is a notarized statement you made to the insurance company's investigator. Read it over carefully." Joel did, very slowly. "Is everything in the statement absolutely accurate, or is there anything in it, no matter how minor, that's incorrect?" I handed Joel a yellow legal pad and pencil. "Read it again, and make whatever notations you need. Then we'll discuss it."

Joel reread it, made a few notes, and looked up. "Just one small thing. It says I had nothing to drink. That's not quite right. I had one light beer with dinner."

I smiled. "What brand?"

"Miller Light, that's what I usually order."

"How'd it come?"

Joel looked up, puzzled.

"How was it served—in a bottle, a can, or a glass from the tap?"

"They only carry bottles. I almost always order Miller, but they also have Bud Light, and some times they're out of Miller, so I take what they have."

I pursed my lips. "What size bottle did you get?"

"They only carry twelve ounces."

"That's two glasses. Did you finish both?"

Joel had a sheepish expression. "Maybe I shouldn't tell them I had anything to drink."

I shook my head. "Bad idea! Tell them nothing but the truth. The worst thing you can do in litigation is to be caught in a lie. If you're asked whether you had any alcoholic beverages, you will tell them you had one twelve-ounce bottle of light beer. That's the amount you always have at the club, isn't it?"

"Yes."

"Were you feeling it?"

"Not at all."

"Then there's no problem." We continued to discus the case and what he might be asked. He seemed a pretty good study and I concluded, "Joel, there are certain absolute rules for a witness in a deposition. The first one I've already told you. Always tell the truth and nothing but the truth. The second rule is, never volunteer *anything*. The purpose of a deposition is to give the other side material they can use against you at the trial. For that reason you should only answer the questions you're asked. Under no circumstances should you volunteer any information not asked for in a question. If Mr. Ayala wants a hundred pieces of information, you must make him ask a hundred questions. Third, if you don't understand a question, don't try to answer it. Say you don't understand, and I'll have the lawyer rephrase it. Fourth is, if you don't know the answer to a question, say you don't know, and don't be afraid of saying that as often as you need to. And finally—you must pay attention to what *I* do or say. If I speak up during your testimony, *immediately* stop talking. If I instruct you not to answer a question, don't. Those are the rules. Do you understand them?"

Joel nodded.

Maybe I should have been a teacher, I thought.

AT 11:30 THE INTERCOM BUZZED. Ayala and the reporter had arrived. "Send them up," I said to the receptionist, "and order another coffee and cookie service."

A few minutes later they appeared. Ayala was, as usual, impeccably attired in a light-blue-checked summer suit. The reporter was a dumpy woman with badly dyed blonde hair, in her late forties, wearing a dress that looked like it had come from a thrift shop.

Ayala bounded into the room and shook hands with Alex and me. "Thanks for the use of your facilities. My suite has too many offices for one conference room."

"You're welcome, Miguel." I stretched my palm toward Joel, who was seated on his right. "This is my client, Mr. Berger. Joel, this the plaintiff's attorney, Mr. Ayala."

As we shook hands, a maid came in with coffee, butter cookies, china cups, and saucers.

Ayala smiled. "Very fancy. I must get invited here more

often."

I turned to my associate, seated on my left. "Alex, remind me to invite Mr. Ayala to our victory party."

Ayala chuckled as Alex made a note on his legal pad. The lawyer handed the reporter a copy of the examination notice so that she could copy the caption, while everybody helped themselves to coffee and cookies.

Then the reporter, who was also a notary public, administered the oath to Joel, and Ayala started.

He identified Joel as the defendant, and asked him about his occupation and his experience in being deposed, which was nil. He asked if Joel had been involved in an automobile accident on October 10 of the previous year, to which Joel answered, "Yes, but it was no accident."

Ayala jumped in with both feet. "How fast were you driving when you intentionally or recklessly crashed into the rear of the automobile in which the plaintiff was a passenger?"

This was so stupid, I thought. "Mr. Berger, did you understand that question?" I asked.

"I didn't," Joel replied, looking shocked.

I turned to Ayala. "Counselor, are you here to get information or play games? If you want information, ask a proper question. If you don't, let's end this charade now."

"What's wrong with the question? I'm entitled to know how fast he claims he was driving."

"Then ask proper questions."

"Well, what do you want me to ask him?"

"That's for you to decide, but if you want information don't ask loaded questions that neither my client nor I understand. If you're really interested in the forward speed of the defendant's automobile at the time the two cars met, ask it."

"Are you directing your client not to answer the question?"

"If he doesn't understand it, how can he answer it?"

"He obviously does understand the question. Since he says it was not an accident, he must have crashed into my client's car either intentionally or recklessly."

The man was *so* predictable and I snickered as I shook my head. "Those aren't the only alternatives. You left out the one that actually happened."

"And what was that?"

"That the driver of the car, in which the plaintiff was a passenger, intentionally backed into the defendant's automobile."

Ayala laughed. "Cut the crap. That never could have happened. If you don't believe me, ask the judge."

My eyebrows rose. "Really, Miguel? I didn't know he was one of your witnesses. I didn't see his name on the police report."

"Very funny. Okay, I'll let your client tell his phony

story so I can tear it apart on trial, but I still want to get a ruling on my question."

I shook my head. "Do what you please, but how can you get a ruling on a question that's been answered?"

"Answered? How?"

"He said he didn't understand the question."

At that point, the plaintiff's attorney geared his questions to how the defendant claimed the accident had happened. When he was finished, I asked, "Are you really going to pursue your motion for a protective order? You know I'm entitled to examine the plaintiff."

"Not with Judge Robbins," Ayala replied. "And I'm going to get my ruling on a perfectly proper question you told your client not to answer."

"You and I are going to spend a lot of time in the appellate division," I retorted, as Ayala and the reporter trooped out of the room.

After they left, Joel turned to me "I'm confused."

"How come?" I asked. "You did very well."

Joel smiled. "He asked about liquor in the car, but wasn't he supposed to ask me how much I had to drink at dinner?"

I grinned broadly. "He should have. I guess he forgot."

CHAPTER SIXTEEN

THE NEXT MORNING, I CALLED ALEX into my office. "What's up?" the big man asked.

"Look, Alex, as you know, the Ramos motion for a protective order is on for this coming Wednesday."

"Yes?"

"I'm sure that, as outrageously wrong as it is, the judge is going to grant it, because he thinks that the threat of going to trial without any disclosure or discovery will force us to settle."

Alex nodded.

"And we've got to build a record so the appellate division will take the case away from him for the second trial."

". . . What do you have in mind?"

"It wouldn't surprise me if, at the call of the motion calendar, he continues to demand the presence of the crooked tennis player. I intend to be there."

Alex's smile wavered and I had a guilt twinge.

"Don't be upset—you'll still be handling the motion. I'll step in only if I have to, but more importantly, I think we ought to document what the judge says."

"How can we do that? . . . It's a shame Judge McKenna couldn't let us use his intern for the last motion."

I nodded. "I was mulling it over last night, and I think I have a solution. I don't want to sneak in a recorder, but if we can get a certified shorthand reporter, who uses a steno pad instead of a machine, we can plant her in the courtroom."

"And have her prepare the transcript of the motion calendar," said Alex with enthusiasm. ". . .But how do we *use* it?"

I nodded again. "Another good question. I haven't figured that out yet, but let's get the bullet and then decide how to shoot it. I've heard there are still a few reporters who use pen and paper. Check with the litigation and estates departments, and see if anyone knows who they are. I'll be a useful expense. In any event, Judge McKenna can show it to his friend in the appellate division.

"You know," Alex said with the hint of a smile. "Your being in court may keep the judge from insulting me."

I chuckled. "When the man insults you, speak up. It

may even make it into the record."

"I'll try."

" ... By the way, how're you doing with Herb Phillips's stuff?"

Alex sighed. "I'm reading."

"I know what you mean," I snorted.

I GOT HOME AT 7:30. As the door slammed, I heard Sue's voice: "Daddy's home, Marcia. Go give him a big hug."

I picked up my little girl, and the hug went both ways. How's my little sweetheart?"

"I'm a big girl, Daddy. Gonna get a baby sister."

"You sure are." I carried her into her room and started to hand her to Sue, who pointed to the crib.

"No crib, Daddy. Wanna *bed*."

"I told you," said Sue, "you'll get your bed after your sister comes," .

"What's baby's name gonna be, Mommy?"

"What do you *want* it to be?" Sue asked with a chuckle.

"How about 'Mary,' like Nanna?"

"Nanna would like that, sweetie," I replied, "but Grandpa Sam says that'll make too many Marys, and he's afraid they'll gang up on him. So why don't you try to think of another name you'd like her to have? Maybe you'll dream it."

"Okay, I'll try."

I tucked her in, we both kissed her, and Sue turned on the intercom as we repaired to the kitchen.

"What's cooking?" I asked as she pressed a button on the microwave.

"Beef stew, from Trader Joe's."

"Sounds good—perfect with cabernet."

She shook her head. "Not for you it' not. You're on the wagon till *she* comes out." She pointed to her expanded abdomen

"How am I going to hurt her?"

"By making her mother unhappy.... Come to think of it, I don't care what you do, so long as I don't see it or smell it."

She was still the same good person, he realized—just a little stressed. I raised a palm. "Okay, I promise, but when?"

She let out a breath. "Damned if I know. She's a week late now. My doctor wants to induce if I'm not in labor by Monday, but I'm not so sure."

She was bothered, and my expression sharpened. "What's troubling you?"

"I read somewhere that inducing increases the chance I'll need a C-section."

"I've heard that too, but cooking her too long isn't good either."

"I know. I've got to think about it."

"You'll make the right decision. You usually do. Just keep me in the loop."

She nodded and kissed me.

ON WEDNESDAY MORNING, ALEX AND I were seated in Judge Robbins's courtroom, waiting for the motion to be called. We were number seventeen of twenty-two, and the call at nine when my cell phone vibrated. I left the courtroom, spoke with Sue, returned two minutes later, whispered into Alex's ear, and left again. When the motion was called, both attorneys answered, "Ready." Then Judge Robbins looked up, a vicious smile on his face. "Where'd the crooked tennis player go? He get afraid to face me?"

"Mr. Andrews got an emergency call and had to leave, Your Honor," Alex told him.

"Emergency, my foot. Does that crook think he's too important to be in my court?"

"Your Honor, he just learned that his wife is having an emergency C-section."

The judge's face reddened. "That's a lot of crap! Don't lie to me, sonny."

"It's the absolute truth, Judge," Alex nearly shouted, "and I object to your calling me 'sonny.' My name is Alexander Tietel. I'm an attorney at law, and you should call me Mr. Tietel."

"You're in contempt, kid. Whose motion is this?"

"Plaintiff's, Your Honor," Ayala answered.

"Motion granted. Submit order. Next case."

HALF AN HOUR LATER, THE MOTION CALENDAR was completed, and the judge left the bench. As the courtroom emptied, a small, thin, white-haired woman closed her sten pad, returned it to a large pocketbook, and joined the departing throng.

As Alex left the courtroom, several of the lawyers congratulated him, and one old timer patted him on the back.

CHAPTER SEVENTEEN

I N LESS THAN HALF AN HOUR, I arrived at the waiting area of the obstetrical department at New York Presbyterian. There I paced for the next several hours until Sue's obstetrician came out to congratulate me on the arrival of my second daughter and to assure me that Sue was doing well. She suggested that I'd be able to visit mother and child after I'd had lunch.

Later, I returned one of the many calls from my mother-in-law. "Hi, Mere. Sue came through like the champion she is, and Sylvia looks just like you."

"I see the Jews won this round," Mary replied. "At least you kept it in the family."

"Yes, Sam and my mother won out. You'll get your turn with naming your great-granddaughter. But you know what's really funny? Sylvia, who's named for my side of the family, looks like you, while Marcia, who was named after your mother, is the spitting image of mine."

The next day I started to shop for Marcia's new bed.

JUDGE MCKENNA RETURNED MY CALL late Monday afternoon. "Congratulations! How's your wife?"

"Very well, thank you. I took her home on Sunday. How did you know?"

McKenna chuckled. "My wife's an avid reader of The *Village Voice*. Cover to cover. What's your daughter's name?"

"Sylvia, after my mother."

McKenna chuckled again. "That's my mother-in-law's name. I'll have to take her into my family. . . . But only after she sleeps through the night."

I smiled. "You called it just right, and she is loud."

". . . How can I help you?"

"I'm going to be in the Bronx Wednesday afternoon. May I drop by at the usual hour?"

"My coffee pot and I await you."

AT 5:30 WEDNESDAY AFTERNOON I came through the unlocked entrance door of the judge's chambers. "*Hello*, Judge."

"I'm in my room. Come ahead."

McKenna was seated behind his desk, reading a file and sipping from a cup. "You know where the coffee is. Help yourself and have a seat. . . . One of the things I'm going to miss when I retire is our coffee klatches."

"Me, too. Maybe we can just change the location. My firm and my wife both serve good coffee."

The judge nodded. "You're on. What's up—or should I say, what did my colleague do this time?"

I showed him my motion file, including the official reporter's minutes, the certified shorthand reporter's minutes, and Ayala's proposed order seeking legals for frivolous opposition to the motion.

The judge read the papers, shaking his head. "Tradition has it that Jewish lawyers are supposed to be smart. This character is inviting the scandal we must avoid. . . . But I assume you would like to use it for the benefit of your client."

"I've been thinking about it," I replied somberly.

"May I have copies to show to my contact in the appellate division?"

I handed them to him.

"Let's adjourn this meeting till Friday evening, and don't do anything about it before then."

I checked my diary and nodded.

"In the meantime," the judge asked, "who's the head of your firm's litigation department?"

"Gordon Jones."

McKenna wiped up a few drops of spilled coffee. "He's appeared before me several times, and I've heard good things about him. Talk to him before our meeting—and by the way, you might want to send a copy of your daughter's birth article to Robbins."

"I already have."

LATE THAT FRIDAY AFTERNOON, the judge and I were again in our seats, drinking his coffee. "You get any response from Robbins about the birth story?"

"Nary a word."

"I did. He thinks you were setting him up for a birth gift."

"My God."

"Speak to your partner?"

"Yup."

"And he was against your plan?"

"Strongly."

"He told you it might work short term, but in the long run it'd be a disaster for you and your firm."

My expression showed my puzzlement. "Yeah. You haven't talked to him, have you?"

"No need. It was obvious. You were going to move to re-argue the motion, and use the private reporter's minutes to show that he decided against you because of his prejudice against you."

I nodded.

"And what's it going to get you? He probably won't change his mind on the motion—he's either too stubborn or too stupid to do that—and you'll have to win the appeal in any case. That's the short term benefit, and to get that you'll be a whistle blower. You know how popular that will make you with all the other judges you'll be before in the future . . . and while you're at it, you'll make the Bronx county leader your enemy."

". . .What should I do?"

"Take your appeals. Move to consolidate them, and ask for a new judge. Judiciary Law section 14 won't let them disqualify him, but it won't stop the appellate division from blasting him and recommending that he recuse himself. And while you're at it, some of the paperwork will be passed around in the court system, and to the county leader too, which will make you look like the nice young man you are."

"It's better than nothing—but there must be a way of getting a different judge. The appellate division will see to it that I get my discovery, but I assume Judge Robbins will keep the case for trial rather than send it to a trial part. And I'm sure he'll poison the jury against me."

The old judge nodded. "You're right, but if you protect your record you can upset a plaintiff's verdict on appeal, and *then* the appellate division will send you to a different judge."

I shook my head. "And just how do I protect a record with Judge Robbins editing it to suit himself?"

McKenna smiled. "I think I can help you there. I'm going to call the reporter in, show him what you've given me, and tell him that unless he wants to lose his job and possibly go to jail, he'd better stay on the straight and narrow from here on. My friend at the appellate division has assured me—if there are any further complaints about the record, they'll proceed against him regardless of what County Chairman Williams says."

CHAPTER EIGHTEEN

A T 10:00 ON MONDAY EVENING Gareth Williams was just getting home from his monthly county committee meeting. He had been allowing the meetings to run a little later now that he was no longer in Congress. While there, he'd been a member of the Tuesday to Thursday Club and needed to catch an early Washington flight Tuesday morning. He'd enjoyed his thirty-eight years in the capital, especially the last ten as ranking member of the Ways and Means Committee, but the time had come. While he used his near-ninety years as an excuse for stepping down, everyone knew that the real reason was his fear of losing to a reform Democrat in the primary, so he'd made his deal with the rascals to keep the county leadership in exchange for the congressional seat.

"Kathy?" he called out, as he entered his home on Judge's Row, the nickname for an area in the Northeast Bronx with homes situated half in Westchester County, so office holders could claim Bronx residency while sending their children to Westchester public schools.

"In my room, Dad," came a voice from the second floor. "Meet me in the kitchen," she said. I want a cup of tea before I go to sleep."

As he headed for the kitchen, he watched her glide down the curved staircase. She was the image of her mother, who'd passed away nearly five years before. It seemed that she'd inherited Lane family genes. Lane women were all tall and slim. Her mother and her mother's two sisters had been high school teachers, and Kathy had followed in their footsteps, except that she was on the faculty at Taft, a public high school, while her mother and aunts had taught in the Catholic school system.

Williams men, by contrast were short and pudgy, Gareth having shrunk several inches in recent years from his former five foot eight.

Entering the kitchen, Kathy leaned down and kissed her father on his cheek, then put a K-cup in the coffee maker and lit the stove under the teapot. "How was the meeting? Any earth- shaking decisions?"

He shook his head. "Not even close, but there were

problems."

"Please, Daddy, you know what the doctor said about your weight," she said, wagging a finger at him as he reached for a box of shortbread cookies in the pantry.

"Just one," he replied. "I need it for my disposition."

She shrugged as she set their cups on the round table and sat down. "What were the problems?"

He put the lone cookie on a dish, and sat next to her. "Only one major one—but it concerns you."

"Robbins?"

He nodded. "They're concerned that my protection of the idiot your friend married may cause a scandal and bring down the organization. I'd like to be county leader for a few more years."

She tugged at her silk robe and took a sip of tea. "I know he's a jerk, and he's driving poor Myrah out of her mind, but what's he really done?"

He dunked the cookie into his coffee and ate half. "Plenty. You know how he hates insurance companies. He insists that they settle all of their cases and pay plaintiffs substantial money, and if they don't, he punishes them."

"Doesn't sound like a particularly good judge. . .but Myrah is such a nice person."

He shook his head, eying the remainder of the cookie. "It gets worse, much worse." He filled her in on Robbins' antics in the Ramos case, and showed her the official and unofficial minutes of the last motion hearing.

"My God!" she gasped, blotting tea from her lips. "Changing court records—isn't that criminal?"

"So I'm told, and I'm quite sure that the reporter is being forced to do it by your friend's husband."

"So he's as guilty as the reporter, who's just following his orders."

He nodded. "This could only have happened because I helped and protected him. If it wasn't for me, he'd still be in the civil court, where he should be."

"And I pushed you into it. . . .What are you going to do about it? Somebody's going to report it. Maybe the lawyer for the insurance company—he's the one who discovered the problem, isn't he?"

Williams sighed. "I'm fortunate there. Frank McKenna, the administrative judge who knows him, has urged him not to be a whistle blower. He's a decent fellow and is going along. And Frank is calling in the reporter and reading the riot act to him. He's being told if there's even a *hint* that he's done it again, he'll be fired and prosecuted criminally."

"What can we do? . . . What can *I* do?"

"Convince your friend to make that moron drop the case."

"I'll try," she swore. I'll speak to her again."

He let out a breath, then finished the cookie.

TEN DAYS LATER, KATHY AND HER FATHER were in the

kitchen eating dinner. "How's the sole, Daddy? Not too dry?"

"It's perfect, dear. You've become as good a cook as your mother—even better." As he savored a forkful of fish, he said, "I know this isn't proper dinner discussion, but have you spoken to Myrah?"

She nodded. "I was going to tell you after we had coffee. I told her what you said, and I was very firm with her. Today we had lunch together. She said she came down very heavily on him, and he promised faithfully that he wouldn't push the reporter to change the record, and he'd stop calling the insurance lawyer a crooked tennis player."

"That's good. How about recusing himself from the case?"

"He won't do it. Says he can be fair, and he's just trying to protect the insurance lawyer from getting into trouble with a frivolous defense."

Williams shook his head. "Okay, we'll leave it be for now."

CHAPTER NINETEEN

A MONTH PASSED. I got home at 6:30 and was met at the door by my older daughter, who tackled me at the knees, giggling loudly. I set down my attaché case, picked her up and hugged her. "I tackle you, Daddy. You supposed to fall down."

I pushed my back against the wall, and slid into a sitting position. "Is that better, my star football player?"

She wagged a finger at me. "Too slow."

"Okay, Champ, I'll practice." I dug in my heels and slid back up the wall.

Sue's voice came from the kitchen. "Marcia, send your father in here."

"Yes, Mommy." She looked up. "Put me down. Mommy wants you."

I laughed. "Oh, my God, now I have two bosses." I bowed to the child and put my coat away. Sue was at the kitchen counter emptying a package of frozen broccoli into a microwave cooker. "Too slow, Daddy," she said holding up her face for a kiss.

"What will my boss imbibe before dinner?" I asked.

"Cabernet, but first bring in the princess while the queen cleans up."

After the children were fed, I read Marcia a story in her new junior bed, while Sue changed Sylvia before depositing her in the crib. "Daddy," Marcia complained, "you told the story all wrong."

"How, sweetheart?"

"It's *Goldilocks and the Three Bears*—not the Three Judges."

"I didn't know that." I kissed her good night, and headed to the bar to fix our drinks.

After dinner, we settled down in the living room with coffee laced with brandy. "Still enjoying being a lady of leisure?"

She glared at him. "You try it."

"I don't have the equipment, but it seems you're ready to go back to the wars."

She nodded. "The doctor suggests two more weeks of this, and the pediatrician wants me to bottle some of my breast milk so we can ease Sylvia into formula. . . . It's not that bad. Harvey's arranged to have one of my associates bring me some of my files, and between the phone, computer, and Internet, I've been able to do some work and keep from going crazy, and it got me back into the office rumor mill. "

"Anything interesting?"

"Yes, I heard you were a bad boy."

"Joan Square?"

"I heard you got her pissed off."

I blushed, caught again. "She overreacted. I got her a divorce case from one of my plaintiffs, and I asked if I could be a little involved to give me some variety. She said no saying they were too complicated for a beginner. Then she complained to Gordon that I was trying to steal her business."

"What did he say?"

He read me the riot act and suggested I take up stamp collecting or write spy novels."

Sue chuckled. "Joan tends to overreact, but you *should* watch yourself."

I shrugged. "Anything else interesting?"

"Same old stuff. There *is* something *you'll* be interested in. Gary Edwards sent me your Ramos file. He says, with my absence, he's been too jammed to give it proper attention."

"I'm pleased to be in your hands. What're you doing

on it?"

"I've put together a draft of a motion to consolidate your discovery appeals and request that they be expedited. I'll print up a copy and give it to you in the morning."

"I look forward to reading it. I'd like to move it along."

She shook her head. "Don't get your hopes up on the expedited appeal. The appellate division doesn't like appeals on motions, and expediting them is very rare."

I let out a breath. "Jerry Arthur is getting antsy. The case is costing him too much, even at the reduced rate I've been giving him. I don't want to lose Capital Casualty's business. . . . What good is the consolidation without the expedition?"

She held up a hand. "You need the consolidation in any event. That way the appeals judges see the pattern in Robbins. Besides, you'll probably get the expedited appeal when he does something that puts your case in immediate danger."

I nodded. "Okay, you're the expert. I'm in your hands," and happy to be there I mused.

CHAPTER TWENTY

ON A BEAUTIFUL SUNDAY in late September, we visited the Bronx Zoo. The trip was ordered by Marcia, on the advice of her beloved pre-school teacher. It was Sylvia's first real outing, and Sue got considerable exercise pushing her in the lightweight carriage that had been Marcia's. It was my job to push the stroller, sometimes with Marcia in it.

After a while at the elephant house, Marcia got bored and demanded: "Daddy, I saw enough elephants. Miss Gold said not to miss the monkeys."

"Miss Gold's wish is my command," I dutifully replied.

The ape house turned out to be a big hit, and it engaged my little girl's rapt attention for nearly two hours, but finally my next command came: "Daddy, I'm hungry. Buy me some ice cream."

I was about to obey when Sue looked down at her. "Didn't you forget something, Marcia?"

Our little girl looked up with a puzzled expression.

"When you ask for something," Sue demanded, "what's the magic word?"

Marcia's expression brightened. "*Please*, Daddy, may I have some ice cream?"

"Yes, dear," I replied.

"You see how the magic word works?" Sue added.

As Marcia giggled, I realized that her appetite had triggered mine. "I could use a caffeine fix," I said.

"There's a refreshment stand just a short way down the road from the entrance, and it has some nice outdoor tables," said a passing zoo attendant.

We found the place a few minutes later, and settled down at a vacant table. I took Marcia to the refreshment stand, where she chose a vanilla cone and I brought back two containers of coffee and a cherry danish. Sylvia had to settle for a few slugs from her bottle of formula.

After a while Sue, reading my mood, asked, "Something bothering you?"

"The usual," I said. "your good friend Judge Robbins."

"*Whose* good friend, Mr. Crooked Tennis Player?"

I nearly broke into a full laugh. "You're right. If it were happening to someone else, it'd be pretty funny."

"But he's happening to you. What's he done now?"

"Figured another way to force me to trial without discovery or disclosure."

She shrugged. "Once we win the appeals, you'll get all you need."

"Yeah—well, my new problem is outside of the two appeals you're trying to consolidate. Just before I left the office on Friday we were served with a note of issue demanding a jury and a certificate of readiness. *Robbins* suggested it. I have to move to vacate it, which I'm sure he'll deny. Once it's on the trial calendar, I can't angle for disclosure or discovery without the judge's permission."

She shook her head. "Fat chance—and you're right, our appeals don't cover that." She thought for a moment. "... But you know, he may have accidentally helped you."

FIRST THING MONDAY MORNING, I called Alex into my office, and told him to bring a copy of the note of issue. I was about to give him the rule about vacating it, but changed my mind. Alex was a good researcher, and was becoming valuable to me. Spoon-feeding him would be an insult. "We have a date," I said instead, "to coordinate with Sue and the appeals department."

Ten minutes later, we were in Sue's office. It was identical to my own, except she'd gone along with the firm's standard curved desk. It was also a lot tidier. I was proud that I had yet again defeated my secretary's neatness campaign.

Seated in a visitor's chair was a thin woman with long dark hair who, even with thick horn-rimmed glasses, was strikingly pretty. Alex gave her an appraising look.

Sue waved us into the remaining chairs. "Bill, this is my associate, Eliza O'Neil—and I assume you're Alex Tietel? Bill and I have discussed the problem, and we're in agreement. If they can keep the case on the trial calendar, they'll be able to drive us to trial blind. We're sure Judge Robbins will refuse to authorize further discovery or disclosure, and you'll be stuck with only the near-useless deposition of the plaintiff."

"Then how does their putting the case on the trial calendar help us?" Alex asked.

"Good question." Sue thumped her index finger on the desk, then pointed it up. "By proving to the appellate division that the judge has a blatant pattern of unfairness, and the emergency of a pending trial, will almost guarantee the consolidation, and expedition, and granting of our soon-to-be three appeals. What I want you two to do is prepare a draft of the motion to vacate the note of issue, documenting the judge's unfair denial of discovery and disclosure. It must be polite—no four-letter words—but firm and clear. Bill will review it, but I'll have the final say."

I smiled, gratified for her ability to take charge.

We all nodded, and Sue turned to her associate. "Lizzy, check with Harvey's secretary and have her dig up all appeals files involving trial calendars."

CHAPTER
TWENTY-ONE

S UE'S GAME PLAN WORKED exactly as she had predicted. As soon as Judge Robbins denied the motion to strike the case from the trial calendar, she
appealed and moved to consolidate all three appeals and
expedite them. Since keeping the case on the trial calendar
created the emergency she needed, the appellate division
gave her what she wanted.

This put Ayala in a bind. Seeing his timing advantage
quickly evaporating, he reached out to his referring attorney. It was 10:00 in the morning one sunny day when the
young lawyer parked his Lexus at a meter on 150th Street
in the Bronx and walked the two blocks to his meeting at
the storefront law office of Carlos Ortiz, Esq., girding himself for the coming confrontation and the knowledge that

it wasn't the best neighborhood in which to park an expensive automobile.

As he passed the bodega next door, Ayala spotted his pudgy host seated behind the front window desk, reading a Spanish newspaper. Before he reached the door, Ayala tapped on the window, and Ortiz looked up and waved.

"How are you, Maria?" Ayala asked the dark-haired slip of a secretary as he reached her desk.

"Very well, Miguel—or should I call you Señor Ayala?"

He bent down and kissed her on the cheek. "Miguel it will always be. Who taught me to be a lawyer?"

"Maria," Ortiz called out, "Señor Ayala is my guest. Send him to me and bring us some of your special coffee."

"Her master's voice." She pointed to Ortiz's front room door.

As Ayala entered, the older man rose and stuck out his hand. "It's been too long, Miguel. Remember when it was every day, before you became a world-famous trial lawyer?"

Ayala smiled at the line of bullshit. "From your mouth to God's ears. . . . Carlos, we've got to talk."

Ortiz held up a palm. "Coffee first."

Ayala nodded. Coffee, well sweetened, came minutes later and coffee and small talk continued for another fifteen minutes.

"Why're you looking at your watch? You have more important things to do?"

"No, my meter's nearly run out."

Ortiz shook his head. "You should have put it in a garage, . . . and in this neighborhood, street parking's not smart."

"I know, but I didn't think it would take this long."

Ortiz's expression brightened. "Don't worry, it shouldn't. What did you want to see me for?"

Ayala's face tightened. "Carlos, you know why I'm here."

Ortiz slowly shook his head. "The witnesses? They're family, just out of town for a while."

"I need them *now*. The appeals have been expedited, and the defendant's going to win them. I need names, addresses, and witnesses to prep *now*."

"Stop worrying, you'll have them."

As Ayala left his referring attorney's office, Ortiz called to his secretary, "Maria, have my aunt get in touch with Raymondo. Tell her that if he wants his money, he's got to be back in town *now*."

When Ayala reached his car, he found a ticket on the windshield and his four fancy hubcaps missing.

TWO WEEKS LATER AYALA CALLED ORTIZ and told the secretary he had to see her boss immediately. "I'm sorry, Miguel, but Mr. Ortiz had to go out of town. His mother-in-law is very ill. She's in a nursing home in San Juan, and he's not sure how long she'll last. He'll be away at least a week. Do you want his phone number?"

He let out a breath. "No, I don't want to talk about it on the phone. You going to be in the office all day tomorrow?"

"Yes, from nine to five. Why?"

"I'm going to be in court in the Bronx tomorrow. Can I drop over and see you when I'm finished?"

"Why? I'm not a lawyer."

He nearly chuckled. "You haven't got a license, but you have a lot more common sense than your boss."

". . . This have anything to do with Raymondo?"

"Everything."

"See you tomorrow."

AYALA WALKED ALMOST A MILE from the Bronx County Courthouse to Ortiz's office. The secretary rose from her desk and presented her right cheek for the traditional kiss.

"You're looking good—nice outfit," he said. The red dress set off her dark hair nicely.

"You know what to say. Wait in Mr. Ortiz's office. I'll make some coffee. Then we can talk." She pointed to a folder on Ortiz's otherwise bare desk. "This is our Ramos file. I think you might want to look it over." She left the room, returned ten minutes later with two steaming cups, and seated herself behind the desk. She took a sip and stared into Ayala's eyes. "You never saw that file, we never had this meeting, and nothing we say was ever said."

He nodded. "Okay—but why are we *doing* this?"

"Because Carlos is like a second father to both of us. He's always been an honorable man, like his father, the chief *abogado* of San Juan. Then his maybe-third cousin, Raymondo, comes along and sells him a bill of goods that he's going to make him a rich man. I assume you spoke to Raymondo."

Ayala nodded slowly and compressed his lips. "He called me yesterday. That's why I'm here. He wants a ten-thousand-dollar cash advance on his piece of the deal. Says he'll call me in a week, and if I have it, he'll come in with his witnesses and help me."

"And when you get caught, you and Carlos will lose your licenses and maybe go to jail."

". . . So what do we do?" Ayala asked in exasperation. "If he promised Raymondo seven percent of the deal—and come to think of it, is that on just the legals or the whole thing?"

"I don't know," she replied, sipping her coffee.

"I learned about it from the file, too. The memo just says seven percent. Did Raymondo tell you anything more?"

He shook his head. They were silent for a few moments, then Ayala furrowed his brow. "I was just thinking," he said. "The defendant says it was a staged accident—that our guy's car intentionally backed into him. I thought it couldn't be, and the judge thinks it's nonsense, but with scum like Raymondo, I don't know. Could Carlos be involved in that, too?"

She shook her head vigorously. "*Never*! He'd never do that. The fee splitting he could think of as cutting corners, but that's *criminal*."

"I agree. He'd never do it. If that's what *Raymondo* did, I'm sure he didn't tell Carlos. . . . But what do *I* do?"

"I've been thinking about that since you called. You've got to talk to Carlos, but only tell him what Raymondo said, and you leave it up to him to swear it isn't true."

"What do I say to Raymondo when *he* calls?"

"Tell him he's got to talk to Carlos."

"And if Carlos admits the deal, and pushes me to join in?"

She took in a big breath. "*Madre de Dios*—I don't want to even think about that!"

CHAPTER TWENTY-TWO

THE APPEAL WAS DECIDED PROMPTLY and unanimously in favor of my defendant. As Judge McKenna had predicted, the decision strongly recommended that Judge Robbins recuse himself from the case, but it stated that, regrettably, the statute didn't authorize them to replace him. Immediately upon being served with the order, Ayala barged into Ortiz's office and shoved it in the man's face. "Carlos, we can't wait any longer. I need to have the names and addresses of the witnesses now, and I've got to prep them."

Ortiz read the order slowly, then looked up. "Calm down, Miguel, I'm working on it. As I told you before, my cousin has some financial problems. I promised I'd help him out when I got my fee in the case, but he has this crazy idea that he's getting a percentage of the fee. I've been trying to straighten him out through the family, but I'll need more time to do it and get his cooperation. Why don't you apply to the Court of Appeals?"

Ayala gritted his teeth. "I'll do that, but if we don't get this on track soon, the judge will have to dismiss the case—and that'll cause us a serious malpractice problem."

ORTIZ'S SUGGESTION WAS CORRECT IF NOT ETHICAL. Ayala applied to the appellate division, which promptly turned him down, and then to the Court of Appeals, which did the same. It bought him over a month's delay, though, and enabled Ortiz to gain the cooperation of the three witnesses.

Two weeks after Ayala was served with the final order, Alex nearly sprinted into my room. "Bill, we got the discovery, he gave us the names and addresses of his witnesses."

I read the document, pulled a form book, and compared Ayala's response to the book's. "It looks right, if it's true."

"You don't think he'd—"

"You *trust* him?" I smiled wondering how many honest adversaries Alex would be likely to meet in his career.

"Guess not. What do you want me to do?"

"Prepare notices of examination before trial for the plaintiff and each of the witnesses, And I want it held here. Include a list of documents they should bring, and make it exhaustive. We're also going to need a Spanish interpreter. Check with the litigation department and find out who they use. I want their best one. Let me see what you've got by tomorrow."

"We going to need an interpreter for *all* of them? Someone knew enough English to talk to the cops."

I shrugged. "Who knows? We'll certainly need one for the plaintiff, and it might be a good idea to keep one in the wings for the witnesses."

"Shouldn't we notice the plaintiff for the nursing home?"

"No. For here. If Ayala wants it there, let *him* ask *us*."

TEN DAYS LATER, I CALLED AYALA. "To what," he asked, "do I owe the pleasure of a call from a big firm partner and tennis crook?" It sounded like he was drinking coffee.

"Cut the crap, Miguel. What are you looking for, an ethics complaint?"

". . .What the fuck are you talking about, Andrews?"

"That lying piece of shit you sent me as a discovery response," I barked. "None of your three witnesses are *at* the addresses you gave. One address is an empty lot, and another's a *bodega* ."

"You're kidding. I've *interviewed* those guys, and those are the addresses they gave me."

"I'll fax you a copy of the process server's affidavit that

I intend to use in my next motion to your buddy Robbins. Then you can have a few days to check it out. But if I don't get what I'm entitled to, you know what I'll have to do."

I hoped his coffee had turned cold and stale.

CHAPTER TWENTY-THREE

A WEEK AFTER I SENT HIM the process server's affidavit, Ayala was still unable to supply correct addresses for his witnesses. Ortiz had asked around in his extensive family, but the best he'd heard was a rumor that Raymondo was in the islands—probably Puerto Rico.

I'd had enough, and submitted a motion to demand discovery and a penalty for failure to give it.

Ayala answered that the witnesses had given him the addresses, and he was doing his best to get the correct ones.

I showed up in court the next time, and when motion was called, declared: "For the motion, ready to argue."

The judge looked down at me from the bench. "We'll have a conference in my robing room after the rest of the motions on the calendar are disposed of."

My stomach churned. The sonofabitch was playing games with me again, and I wasn't surprised that the conference didn't happen until an hour after lunch. During one of the breaks, Ayala came up to me almost sheepishly. "I'm sure you realize, don't you, that I didn't *knowingly* give you those phony addresses?"

I gave him a candid look. "I do, Miguel, and don't worry about my bringing an ethics grievance. I know you didn't mean it. But let me repeat some advice I gave you when we first met: I think somebody dumped a staged accident case on you, and you better cover your ass before *someone* in authority tries to take your law license away."

Ayala shook his head. "I don't think so. I've spoken to the witnesses, and they sound genuine."

I shrugged. ". . .If they convince me after I examine them, maybe there'll be some money on the table."

When the conference was called, we joined Robbins, who smiled broadly and stared directly at me. "I guess you're wondering why I called this conference instead of hearing argument in the courtroom?"

"It did cross my mind, Your Honor," I replied, returning the stare, "but I'm sure you'll tell us."

"It was out of consideration to you, Mr. Andrews."

"Oh?"

"Yes, I began to realize that calling you a crooked tennis player in public seemed to embarrass you."

I suppressed a smile. "An interesting thought, Your Honor. I wonder why making accusations about me in open court that you know are false doesn't seem to embarrass *you*."

Ayala gritted his teeth. The judge's mouth tensed. "Very funny."

"Thank you, Your Honor, and please accept my apologies for violating your judicial prerogatives." Seeing a puzzled expression on the judge's face, I added, "Your right to make *all* of the jokes in your court."

He shook his head. "Okay, let's get to your motion. The appellate division says you can have the names and addresses of the witnesses. What seems to be the problem, Mr. Ayala?"

"As I stated in my opposing papers, the witnesses are known to my referring attorney, Mr. Ortiz. He's temporarily lost track of them, and he's actively looking for them through his family connections. We'll need some time to relocate them—but Mr. Andrews' suggestion of a dismissal penalty is draconian."

The judge nodded. "Quite right, I'd *never* do that. How much time will you need?"

"Hopefully, a few months will do it."

"Okay, you're ordered to give the correct names and addresses to the witnesses to the accident within three months."

I locked eyes with the judge. "What's the penalty if he doesn't?"

The judge snickered. "Don't worry, he will."

I kept my voice as even as I could when I asked. "But what if, after three months, he *still* hasn't given me the discovery that the appellate division ordered?"

"We'll talk about it then. Tell the clerk to send in the next conference." Robbins pointedly pushed the case file aside.

AS WE LEFT THE COURTROOM, I turned to my opponent. "Miguel, this case isn't doing either of us any good."

"Why do you say that?"

"I'm doing a ton of extra work for which I have to bill the carrier at a discounted rate in order not to risk losing their business, and even then they're grumbling. And you're doing a lot of extra work for which you're not getting paid at all. The goodies you're getting from the clown back there are just creating delay to getting your money—if you're entitled to it— or a dismissal, which will give you more time to handle profitable cases. I'm sure that, if Robbins tries this case, any plaintiff's verdict you get will be upset on appeal."

A wry smile appeared on Ayala's face. "What do you propose instead?"

I paused in the hallway and studied the tense contours

of his face. "We've got to work together to send the case to someone else," I said at last, "But the only thing I can think of to force the issue could be hurtful to you." Ayala's eyes narrowed. "As you know," I went on, "you can only force the recusal of a judge on family or financial grounds. Since he's not related to either of us, we're left with financial. I think you'll agree that, with the outrageously bad decisions he's made—all in favor of one side, it could look like he's being paid off. The appellate division could look into whether there's a financial basis for removing him. But from your standpoint, the downside is obvious."

"*Hey*! I've never offered the guy *anything*."

I raised a palm. "Of course *you* haven't, but from my standpoint, the crooks who caused the alleged accident *could* have. But that's the only idea I've come up with. Maybe you can come up with a better one."

A crestfallen look flickered in his eyes. "I'll think about it."

As I left the courthouse, I realized I'd have to hurry. I was late for a meeting with my real estate partner, Mort Topper, and some outside attorneys. We were going to discuss the possibility of defending against mortgage foreclosures. I'd have to take a course to get up to speed, but maybe it would give me a new birth of legal freedom.

CHAPTER
TWENTY-FOUR

O N A CRISP FEBRUARY MORNING, Carlos Ortiz was at his desk reading a Spanish newspaper. It only reported local news, but he read it primarily to keep up his bilingual skills. His concentration was interrupted by a loud tapping noise. As he looked up he saw a tall, broad-shouldered man rapping a coin against the storefront window. It was Raymondo, and the lawyer motioned him to come in. He punched the intercom. "Maria, some of your famous coffee for my long-lost cousin, Señor Sanchez."

The big man strode through the door and kissed Maria on both cheeks. "I'm hungry. Get me something to eat with my coffee." He turned, marched into Carlos' office, and sank onto the center visitor's chair.

"How was your vacation on the moon?" Carlos asked.

"I don't do business on an empty stomach," Raymondo told him, keeping his hands firmly planted on his jeans-covered knees.

For the next fifteen minutes the two sat staring at each other in silence, until Maria brought in a tray with coffee and a nut-and-raisin cake she had bought from the *bodega* next door. Raymondo bit into his cake and washed it down with half of his coffee.

Carlos, used to his cousin's ways, lifted his cup in a silent toast and took a small sip.

Twenty minutes later, when the man had devoured the entire cake and drunk two cups of coffee, he looked up at his host. "You've been bothering the whole family to get me here. What the fuck do you want?"

"What I'm entitled to, your *cooperation*."

"What the hell you talking about? We cooperated. Me, Ruben and Carlos went to the lawyer's office. We told him everything about how that white-bread fucker smashed into my car and nearly killed Uncle Juan."

Ortiz was shaking his head. "And you all gave him phony addresses. *You* told him you live in an empty lot, and *Ruben* lives in a *bodega*."

Raymondo frowned. "What's he need our addresses for? He want to come for tea? When he needs us for court, you'll reach out for us."

"He has to give the addresses to the insurance company lawyer."

"What for?"

"Cause the court *said* so. They have the right to subpoena you and take your testimony."

"Shit, no—let him come to the trial."

"The appeals court says he's got to get it."

"And if he don't?"

"They throw out the case, and we get *nada*."

Raymondo glared at him. "And what have I got? A crappy ten grand?"

"That was *my* money I gave you."

"And that was *my* case I gave *you*. . . . Tell you what. Give me another twenty, and I'll think about it." With that, the big man rose, knocking over his cup, which smashed on the hard-wood floor, and stormed out.

As he watched Raymondo pass his window, the lawyer shuddered, beginning to wonder how the accident had really happened.

At one in the afternoon, Maria looked in on her boss to see what he wanted for lunch. She found him looking down at his desk, his chin supported by the crook of his hand. "Hey, *patron*, what's the matter? You look like the whole world fell on you."

He shook his head. "My damned cousin, he's killing me."

"He really your cousin?"

"I don't know. He's supposed to be related through my *tia* Carlotta, but she's not sure if he's really family. He showed up one day and told her he was the son of her dead niece by the same name, but she's never heard *that* Carlotta was ever married or had any kids."

"He don't act like any family I'd want to have. His uncle Juan, *he* part of your family?"

"I don't think so. I never heard of him before Raymondo brought him in on this damned case."

"How come he was here today? I thought you told Miguel you couldn't find him."

"I asked Carlotta to reach out to him. I was hoping to get correct witness addresses the judge ordered Miguel to get for the other side so they can examine them."

She looked straight into his eyes. "And?"

"He says he wants more money before he'll cooperate."

"*More* money? You didn't give him *money* for the case, did you? You can lose your license, and maybe Miguel's, too."

"I didn't *give* him money for the case, I made a loan to a family member."

"How much?"

". . .Ten thousand," he replied with a sheepish look.

"Your wife know about it?" she asked, shaking her head.

"None of your business, busybody."

She uttered a mirthless chuckle. "So she doesn't know. That can get pretty bad."

"You don't know the half of it."

"Worse than the money?"

"Much. The insurance lawyer keeps saying it was a set-up accident, and I'm beginning to wonder if that's what Raymondo did."

"That's criminal. Would your so-called cousin do something like that?"

Ortiz shook his head slowly. "I don't know, but there *was* something going around the family that he did time for, something like fraud I think, when he was in California."

"Oh, my God."

CHAPTER TWENTY-FIVE

TWO MONTHS PASSED FROM THE TIME Judge Robbins ordered Ayala to give me the discovery that the appellate division had awarded me, but I still got nothing. While there was another month to go on the judge's three-month frame, I decided to give Ayala a nudge. My first two calls went unreturned. I sent a certified letter suggesting that he get a phone service that could make outgoing calls. The sarcasm apparently worked: A few days later, Ayala called in a placating tone. "Look, Bill, I'm sorry I have to put both of us through this, but these witnesses are strange. My referring attorney, who's a cousin of Raymondo Sanchez, tells me the man absolutely refuses to give any current addresses."

I couldn't believe it. "Miguel, that's not going to fly. A

month from now, I'm sure Robbins'll give you more time, but that's only temporary. I'm going to have to go back to the appellate division, and they will eventually dismiss the case with a frivolous money ruling—probably out of your pocket."

"I'll try to get you what I can, but I'd appreciate it if you didn't bust my chops."

I had to laugh. "Busting your chops is the kindest thing I can do for you. I'll get you off this crazy loser you have and give you time to make some money."

TWO WEEKS LATER, I WAS AT the Queens County Courthouse. One of the first plaintiff's cases I got when I became a partner had risen to the top of the personal injury trial calendar. I was there for a final settlement conference before the trial judge. The liability was so-so, and the injuries were severe enough to bring an over-a-million-dollar jury verdict, and could get me more substantial referrals. The defendant's insurer was offering only a few hundred dollars as nuisance value, and the judge told their lawyer that, if they didn't come up with an acceptable offer by three that afternoon, he would send the attorneys out to select a jury the following morning. I sent my associate back to the office to check on the availability of witnesses, and, after eating a quick lunch, went to the law library on the sixth floor to read my file for the umpteenth time.

It's one of the places a litigator can make use of otherwise wasted time generated by a trial practice. I headed from the center aisle of the large room, with numerous rows of book- shelves and a line of work tables that users could occupy for their research. Ayala was sitting at one of the tables, impeccably dressed as always in an expensive-looking gray pin-stripe. He saw me, rose, ambled up, and said in a whisper, "I'm glad I ran into you. Let's go outside and have a chat."

We sat on one of the oak benches that lined both sided of the sixth-floor hall and the light glowed dully from inadequate ceiling fixtures. "What's up, Miguel? I gather you have some news."

He nodded. "My referring attorney leaned on his cousin. The man wouldn't allow his address out, but he agreed to be examined—on condition that it's a one-shot deal."

I narrowed my gaze. "What's that mean?"

"You get to examine Sanchez once, on one day. He won't give you his address, and this is in full satisfaction of all your discovery and disclosure rights, and you consent to restoring the case to the trial calendar."

I shook my head. "It won't fly, Miguel. You're offering me ten percent of what I'm entitled to in exchange for my going into trial blind. If you were me, would you take it?"

There was a tight smile on Ayala's lips. "It doesn't matter what I'd do. If you don't agree, Robbins will push it down your throat."

I snickered. "And the appellate division will push it right back out. If you want to submit Sanchez, I'll examine him, and let the court, *including* the appellate division, tell us what we're entitled to." I rose, shook his hand, and returned to the library. Trials can be full of surprises, but Ayala and his people were boring the hell out of me.

I got home just before the children's bedtime, and I was able to give them their goodnight kisses. After dinner we settled down for coffee in the living room. "You picking your Queens jury tomorrow?" my wife asked.

I shook my head vigorously. "No such luck, we settled for six hundred thousand."

She snickered. "Poor baby, that was going to be your first million-dollar verdict . . . but it *does* put money in our pocket."

I nodded and sipped coffee.

"What happened to the foreclosure defense program you and Mort Topper were working on?"

"It died in child birth. We advertised for cases but got no takers. Probably good for Mort."

"Oh?"

"One of his bank clients has started giving him foreclosures. He doesn't think they'd be too happy if he was representing the enemy."

She smirked. "I guess they'd call it conflict of interest .... Can he use you for the bank cases?"

I shook my head. "I asked him." The feeling was hollow, but at least I'd tried. Next time, maybe I could try shooting plaintiffs from a roof top.

CHAPTER TWENTY-SIX

THREE MONTHS LATER, AYALA STILL hadn't complied with the judge's order, nor had he offered up Raymondo unconditionally. I had Alex serve a motion for the discovery the appellate division had given me, and I asked for dismissal. Ayala naturally opposed the motion, claiming I had refused to examine his chief witness and cross-moved to declare the discovery waived and restore the case to the trial calendar without further discovery or disclosure. I replied with exactly what Ayala had offered me and asked for a dismissal.

Before the call of the calendar, I fixed Ayala with an impatient glare. "Miguel, I've lost all my respect for you."

"Sorry," the man replied with an embarrassed expression, "but I had to do *something*."

Robbins smiled broadly when I answered, "Ready for the motion," and said he'd hear argument in his robing room after the completion of the calendar.

At 11:30, we were called. "Great," I said to Alex, "no Bronx lunch today."

I expected to see the judge studying a file so that he could keep me waiting for another fifteen minutes, but Robbins was sitting erect, eyes straight ahead, broad smile on his chubby face. He waved us to seats. "Gentlemen, how nice to see you. I'll miss you when this case is over."

"You might consider adopting us," I replied. "You'd get at least two beautiful granddaughters out of it."

Robbins chuckled. "You've informed me about the arrival of . . .?"

"Sylvia."

Robbins nodded. "I didn't know about her older sister. Why 'at least'?"

"My friend hasn't kept me up to date on his progeny."

"I still come solo, Judge," the man replied.

The judge's smile broadened. "I don't think an adoption would work. My wife could have a problem with a son who's a crooked tennis player."

"That could be easily solved, Judge. You could start by calling me a brilliant and honest lawyer."

"No, I'd rather be telling the truth." Robbins glared at me. "Maybe we should get back to the matter at hand.

What makes you think you can demand all kinds of discovery and disclosure when you refuse to examine a witness offered to you on a silver platter?"

"He came with a bunch of completely unacceptable conditions. Mr. Ayala wants me to examine a witness who won't even tell me his address, and the price for that is to give up all other discovery and disclosure, including my right to examine the other two claimed witnesses to the alleged accident, and enough information so I can do a background check on all of them."

"I can see that you just want me to let the insurance company continue to play games with this case. This man's cross-motion makes a lot of sense. I just may grant it."

"You do that, Judge, the appellate division will have some more interesting reading."

"We'll see," Robbins muttered. "Motion and cross-motion marked submitted." He pointed to the door.

When we returned to the courtroom, I asked Ayala, "Think he's going to grant your cross-motion?"

"Seems that way."

"Unless you want an unpaid appellate practice, it's not going to do you any good."

"What can I *do*? I can't get the guy to testify without the conditions."

"Stop throwing good money after bad and get out of the case."

"And what do I tell my malpractice carrier?"

"You tell 'em the truth, Miguel."

Ayala shook his head. "I'll talk to my referring attorney again—tell him he's got to make the guy testify without conditions."

"What're you going to do if Robbins grants your cross-motion?"

"I'll cross that bridge when I get to it. . . . By the way, how'd you make out on that plaintiff's case you had in Queens? I heard the carrier's a ball buster."

"The judge forced a six-hundred-thousand-dollar settlement. Frankly, I'd have preferred trying it."

At that juncture, the clerk shooed us out.

CHAPTER TWENTY-SEVEN

ARLOS ORTIZ'S SECRETARY PUT DOWN the phone and marched into his office. She yanked the Spanish newspaper he was hiding behind, sat down, planted her elbows on his desk, and dropped her chin to her fists, her eyes riveted on his.

"What the hell do you want?" he demanded.

"When?"

"When what?"

"You know very *well* what I mean. When are you going to talk to Miguel? He's been calling for the last three days."

"I'll talk to him when I have something to tell him. If I talk to him before I reach my damned cousin, he's going to push me to drop the damn case."

"Why *don't* you drop it?" she asked, continuing to glare at him.

His head shook slowly. "I can't. . . . I've got too much invested."

"The ten thousand?"

He nodded.

". . .You don't expect to get that *back*, do you?"

"If we get some money from the insurance company."

"If the man won't cooperate, how can you? . . . Be smart, *padron*, drop the damned case before you and Miguel lose your licenses and go to jail."

"I'd like to, but that man makes me nervous. He's one bad *hombre*. . . . Tell you what, get me my Aunt Carlotta. Maybe she can talk some sense into him."

AT SIX THAT EVENING, MYRAH ROBBINS arrived home carrying a shopping bag with that night's dinner. "Harry, I'm home."

"*Yeah*," he growled from the living room.

She put the bag down on the kitchen counter and joined her husband, who was seated in the brown leather recliner, a nearly empty wine glass in his hand. As she pecked him on the cheek, she could smell the alcohol. "Been home long, dear?" she asked as she attempted to remove the half-empty bottle of cabernet from the cocktail table next to him.

"Leave it, I'm not done," he muttered.

"Yes, you are. You've had too much already," she replied, remembering that they had finished the last bottle the night before. "I've brought in Greta's beef stew, and you'll be too drunk to enjoy it."

"Oh, alright." He allowed her to replace the bottle in the bar and lead him into the kitchen.

Dinner was far from festive. Myrah's attempts at conversation were met either by monosyllabic replies or, in one instance, stony silence. By the time dessert and coffee were on the table, she could stand it no longer. "Damn it, Harry, what's eating you?"

"Nothing you could help with."

"Try me," she replied through gritted teeth.

He grunted. "I had to fire my law secretary."

"*Thelma Chan?* . . . She's been with you from the beginning. You've always told me she was the greatest."

He shrugged. "Yeah, she's okay . . . competent."

"What happened?"

"I can't deal with disloyalty."

"What did she do?"

"You wouldn't understand."

She glared at him. "I understand that you just fired the daughter of the president of the lady's division of a Democratic club, whom you hired on the recommendation of the Democratic County leader, who got you your judgeship—so I repeat, *what did she do?*"

He snorted. "It's about that damn insurance lawyer, the tennis player. He got some reversals from the appellate division of some of my orders he claims denied him discovery and disclosure, and that I allowed the case on the trial calendar too soon. So the plaintiff's lawyer gives him the discovery, which he claims was defective, and he makes another damn motion. Then I learn that the plaintiff's lawyer offered him his chief witness for examination, and the man turned it down based on some phony excuse."

"What was the excuse?"

"Oh, he claimed there was a condition that it would satisfy all his disclosure and discovery needs and the case would go back on the trial calendar."

"Sounds like a pretty bad condition."

He shrugged. "What does that insurance company need it for their phony defense? . . . In any event, I decided that if they turned down disclosure, I wasn't going to let them drag their feet, so I told Chan to draw up a decision ending defendant's discovery and putting the case back on the trial calendar in the same position it was when the appellate division knocked it off."

"And what did Thelma do?"

"She wrote a decision granting the defendant's motion and directing the unconditional examination of the plaintiff's key witness. And when I yelled at her, she told me I was out of my mind, and that if she did what I told her to do, the appellate division would reverse it and make me look bad. So I told her she wasn't the judge and she'd better do it my way, and when she stamped her foot and refused, I fired her."

Myrah shook her head in disgust. "She should be the judge. Give me your phone."

He grudgingly handed it to her, and she punched in one of his favorite numbers. "Hello, Thelma. . . . Yes, it's Myrah. How are you, dear? . . . Yes, I know what my stupid husband said. Please ignore it, and tomorrow you can work out that decision properly. . . . You're welcome. Say hello to your mother."

A WEEK LATER, I WAS RETURNING from court when Alex caught me at the water cooler. "You believe in miracles?"

"Gee, I don't know. Did you join a church or something?"

"Even stranger. Robbins just ruled in our favor."

CHAPTER TWENTY-EIGHT

Two weeks later, the phone rang in the Ortiz law office. "Carlos, it's Miguel—he's returning your call." He put his Cuban cigar down on the ashtray. "Hello, Miguel, thanks for your promptness. . . . Yes, I know it should go both ways, and, in the future, I'll try to do that. . . . Yes, he contacted me, and better still, he's agreed to show up for his examination. Call me when you agree on the date. . . . Conditions? I don't know what's going through the guy's head, but he didn't mention any to me this time. " He picked up the cigar and took a deep drag. Things seemed to be going better.

A week went by. I asked Capital for some investigative help on the case and Mark Stevens sent Charlie DiNapoli. Alex and I met the investigator in one of the small conference rooms. As usual, there was a coffee and cookie service on the blond wood table. Charlie dressed for the occasion in a blue blazer, striped shirt, and tie. "Good meeting you at last, Mr. Andrews, Mark Stevens has been singing your praise to the skies."

"He's very high on you too, and your reports on the Ramos case are very impressive. . . . By-the-way, my father was Mr. Andrews, I'm Bill."

"First names, just like Capital, fine with me. How can I help you Bill?" He nibbled on a cookie and smiled. "These are good, I'll have to come here more often."

"We like to feed our guests so long as Mark okays the time charges." I reached over to Alex who pushed a file to me. I extracted a copy of Joel's deposition transcript and several copies of his affidavits, and handed them over. "I assume you've seen these?"

The investigator skimmed the papers for the next five minutes, then looked up and nodded. "I'm fully familiar with them."

"Then you know that our defendant insists that the so-called accident was staged by the other driver?"

"Yes, and I believe him."

"So do I. . . . Up to now, they've refused to give us accurate information about this driver other than that his name is Raymondo Sanchez, and that he claims to be a nephew of the plaintiff. We now have his examination before trial scheduled, and the plaintiff's attorney has agreed to produce him."

"That's great. When you get enough information on him, I'll be able to do a thorough investigation and hopefully dig up some dirt. I assume you don't need my advice on what questions to ask or what documents to ask for?"

"That's not my problem. I'm sure that all he'll testify to are the alleged facts of the accident, and when I try to get information about him, he'll either refuse or tell me lies. What I'll need is physical information so that we can find out who he really is."

"Like finger prints and DNA?"

"Precisely, but asking him directly isn't going to get me anything."

"So what you want from me is help in running a sting?"

"That about sums it up."

"I've never run one, but I think some of my buddies from the force have. What's your time frame?"

"It's scheduled for two weeks from yesterday."

"I'll get back to you in a few days."

THREE DAYS LATER, I PAID A LATE AFTERNOON visit to my partner Gordon Jones. "I see neither of us is in line for the firm's neatness award."

"I thought Edna's project—" Jones was referring to my secretary—"had removed you from the manly slob club."

I shook my head. "She tried, but I couldn't live with it."

Gordon took a final sip of his scotch on the rocks, and pointed to the tray on the only clear end of his desk, on which stood a bottle of twelve-year-old Dewar's, an ice bucket, and two glasses. "Please pass me the bottle after you pour yours, then you can tell me how I can otherwise assist you."

We sipped companionably for a few minutes as I mused on what a good guy my partner was. Then I forced myself back to business. "You recall my Ramos case?"

"How could I forget it?"

"It's about to go cloak-and-dagger."

"How exciting, maybe we can turn it into a best-seller."

"Any thing's better than what we've got. My problem is to get personal information from someone who won't give it."

"The driver of the plaintiff's car?"

"Correct. His lawyer agreed to produce him for examination in a couple of weeks, but I'm sure he won't give me anything that'll help me get some dirt on him. Capital's investigator, DiNapoli, suggested how we can get pictures, finger prints, and possibly DNA surreptitiously, but I'll need a conference room with a one-way mirror or its modern equivalent. Do we have such an animal? Charlie says he knows of someone who can equip a room with sound and viewing equipment."

"Check with Willie Smith in the managing partner's office. If we don't have it, get me a cost estimate, and I'll push it through the executive committee."

Good old Gordon, I can always count on him.

CHAPTER
TWENTY-NINE

EARLY IN THE EVENING NINE DAYS LATER, Charlie, Joe Regan, a former police detective, and I entered a small interior office of the Franklin firm outfitted with six monitors each showing a different view of a middle-sized conference room, half a floor away. It was furnished with a table that would seat twelve, although the only occupant was Alex Tietel. Each of the chairs had a paper number taped to the back. Charlie's voice came over the intercom: "Alex, sit in seat number one, look toward the table, and smile for the birdie. . . . Okay, the picture came out great, and you're very photogenic. Now go to seat number two." After he had been photographed in each numbered seat, and in several other parts of the room. Alex changed places with me and we ran the test again.

We then settled down in the conference room. Charlie complemented Regan. The burly man with thick, curly salt-and-pepper hair smiled appreciatively.

"So no question we can get pictures of the guy. What about fingerprints and DNA?" Charlie continued.

"You buy the paper cups and plates I suggested?"

"Yeah," I replied. "And they're nice and decorative."

"So long as the subject puts a hand on either a cup or plate, you'll get great prints, but the crew in the observation room will have to watch him like hawks so you know exactly which cup or plate's his."

"We'll have one man at each monitor, and we want you there to take care of any problem with the equipment. What about DNA?"

"That's iffy. You could get some from skin oil or maybe saliva, but I wouldn't count on it."

"Okay," I concluded. It's the best we can do. I'll look forward to seeing you gentlemen in two days."

Aᴘʀɪʟ 27 ᴡᴀs ʙʀɪɢʜᴛ ᴀɴᴅ sᴜɴɴʏ, but that morning Alex, the court reporter and I were cooling our heels in window-less Conference Room C. The Sanchez deposition had been scheduled for nine-thirty, but neither Ayala nor the witness had appeared or called. I'd phoned the lawyer several times; each time I'd been told the man was out. By 10:30, I'd been about to take their default, and maybe play hooky and take Marcia to the park, when the intercom buzzed. "He's on his way," I announced, and twenty minutes later they arrived. Ayala was, as always, immaculately dressed, this time in a blue pin-striped suit. Raymondo was wearing jeans and a dark, heavy winter jacket.

"Sorry for the delay, Andrews. Mr. Sanchez hadn't had breakfast," said Ayala as he shook my hand.

"There's plenty to eat here, Mr. Sanchez," I replied pointing to a sideboard with a coffee urn and several fancy paper plates loaded with pastries and cookies.

"I can always eat more," said Raymondo, ignoring my outstretched hand as he made for the food, where he took coffee and a serving plate full of Danish, sat down, took off his jacket and dug in.

Fifteen minutes later, I turned to Ayala "Can we get started?"

As Raymondo returned to the conference table with more coffee and another full serving dish, his lawyer whispered into his ear.

"Don't worry," the big man boomed, "I can eat and talk."

"Okay, Cora," I said to my reporter, a frizzy-blonde, who looked like she might explode out of her knit slacks, "please swear Mr. Sanchez in."

"*Swear* me in? What's *that* about?" boomed the big man, flexing his biceps so that the skulls tattooed on them seemed to smile.

I rose, and turned to him. "Mr. Sanchez the rules require that you testify under oath."

Raymondo stood glowering at me. "Fuck the rules, the mother fucker ran his car into the back of my car and almost killed my Uncle Juan. That's my testimony." He put his jacket back over his Hawaiian shirt and turned to Ayala. "Let's go."

"Wait a minute," said the lawyer, grabbing the man on his shoulder, but Raymondo pushed it off and stomped out of the room.

"I'll try to bring him back," said Ayala as he followed his witness.

I turned to the reporter, who was busy typing. "You get it all down?"

"Every word."

Fifteen minutes later the intercom buzzed, it was Ayala. "Yes, Miguel. . . . Thanks, I'll see you in court."

"I guess he won't be back," said Alex.

"You got it. He said the man disappeared into thin air. Now let's see if we can identify every fingerprint and maybe get some DNA."

CHAPTER THIRTY

ENTLEMEN, WHAT A PLEASURE to see you again," said a broadly smiling Judge Robbins as he waved us to seats in his robing room. Conferences there had become his modus operandi in preference to hearing argument on Ramos motions in open court.

"The pleasure is mutual, Your Honor," I replied, I was in no mood to provoke another dispute.

"So what have we here?" said the judge, looking directly at Ayala.

"It's Mr. Andrews' motion, Your Honor."

As Robbins turned towards Bill, his smile faded. "What're you bothering me with today, Mr. Andrews?"

I would have liked to tell the judge that it was all in his papers, but I went along with the game. I opened the folder on my lap and pretended to skim my copy of the motion papers, which I actually knew nearly by heart, then I looked up at the judge. "Your Honor, three weeks ago Mr. Ayala brought Raymondo Sanchez, the driver of the plaintiff's car, for his examination before trial."

"Was that pursuant to a notice?"

"Yes, Judge." I laid the open folder before him and pointed to the notice and the proof of service of the notice.

The judge pretended to read. "Yes, they seem in order. What's the problem?"

I tightened my jaw trying to suppress my newly learned anger. "My affirmation in support of the motion, which I'm sure you've read, shows that Mr. Sanchez refused to be sworn and left without testifying."

The judge's smile broadened to a near grin. "But, according to the reporter's transcript, he did testify. The language may have been a little strong, but it tells it all. What more can you possibly need?"

"...It's not under oath, and I would want details about the witness—such as his address, his criminal record, his relationship to the plaintiff, where he picked up the plaintiff, and the course of events that preceded the alleged accident among many other things."

Robbins shook his head. "Unnecessary details. The man is apparently a little simple. I'm sure you can get the details you want by cross-examining him before the jury at trial." He turned to Ayala. "Counsel, I assume you can get the witness to swear to his testimony."

"I'll try, Judge," replied Ayala who was visibly shocked.

"I'll re-read the papers and decide this obviously frivolous motion in a few days." Robbins pointed to the door.

"I'm sure the appellate division will enjoy reading your decision," I remarked dryly.

"Don't you *dare* threaten me!" the judge shouted.

At the conclusion of the motion calendar, Robbins returned to his chambers and barged into his law secretary's minute interior room. On hearing him enter, the thin Asian woman turned from her computer. He dropped the motion calendar with his comments in the middle of her desk. "Here's a new batch of decisions for you to write."

He waited as she read over his notations and looked up. "What about Ramos?"

He looked back at her with a puzzled expression. "What about it?"

"There are no notations. I assume you're going to grant the motion. My only question would be the penalty. Dismissal of the action with prejudice might be a little harsh."

He glared at her. "You must be kidding. Deny the motion and access a frivolous penalty and legals."

A WEEK LATER, AS MYRAH ROBBINS GOT home from school, she picked up a ringing phone. "Hello. . . . Oh, it's you,

Thelma.... I'm glad you enjoyed the flowers, you certainly earned them.... I know you tried to have him recuse himself, but if he did that Mr. Williams would have nominated you for sainthood." Both women were laughing as they hung up their phones.

That evening, at the offices of Franklin Powers and Rush, Alex caught me in the men's room. "Guess what."

I chuckled. "You won the lottery, you're starting a new firm, and you want to hire me as your junior clerk."

"That'll be the day. No, it's about Ramos. We sort of won the motion."

"Sort of?"

"Yeah, he granted the motion, and directed Sanchez to be examined under oath within thirty days of the service of the order."

"And if he doesn't comply with the order?"

"It doesn't say."

I shrugged as I adjusted my clothing.

"GET ME A CUBAN SANDWICH and a *cervesa*," Raymondo demanded, after barging into the store-front office and pounding on Maria's desk, "and make it quick, I'm hungry."

He turned, stomped into Ortiz's room, grabbed the lawyer's tie, and pulled him to his feet. "What the fuck *you* want?"

The older man landed on his chair which rolled into the credenza behind his desk as Raymondo released the tie and shoved his chest. "What're you, nuts?" he gasped. "Put your hands on me again, and I'll call the cops and have you arrested,"

"You do that, and you won't live to see them." The big man removed a hunting knife from inside his right boot and pointed it at Ortiz. "Now, why you bothering my aunt?"

"Only way to reach you."

"Okay, I'm here, what you want?"

"The ten thousand I loaned you."

"What loan? That was a down payment for getting you a great case that your man is fucking up."

"That case is worth shit unless you work with him. Now, you either cooperate with Miguel or give me back my money."

Raymondo sat down, replaced the knife in his boot, put his elbow on the desk, and with his chin on his hand stared into Ortiz's eyes. After a minute he looked up, turned his head to the window and saw Maria returning from the *bodega* with a bag in her hand. "I'll think about it," he said as he rose, intercepted her, grabbed the bag, and departed.

FIVE WEEKS AFTER THE ORDER WAS SERVED on Ayala, I called him. I knew it would be a waste of time having Alex make the call since the plaintiff's lawyer only responded to higher authority.

I was right; the man returned my third call. "To what do I owe the honor?"

I tasted my digestive juice. The son-of-a-bitch was getting to me, but I kept my cool. "Remember the last order?"

"It was so memorable, how could I forget it?"

"Well, this is advance notice that I'll be making a motion to dismiss your complaint for failure to obey the umteenth disclosure order."

"You wouldn't do a nasty thing like that—would you?"

"With the greatest of pleasure."

"Seriously, Bill, please. Hold up for a week. Carlos is working on the man, and I think I'll be able to schedule an examination by then."

A WEEK WENT BY. I received an envelope from Ayala with a signed stipulation adjourning the examination before trial of Raymondo to a blank date, and a letter asking him to call and agree on the date. I complied, and we agreed.

At the end of the call Ayala said, "my man made a couple of conditions."

". . .Oh?" I said, feeling a throb in my temple.

"He's agreed to be sworn, but he won't say what questions he'll answer."

"We'll let your buddy with the black robe rule on that, of course, subject to appeal."

"Fine, and one other thing. He wants more of the goodies you served him last time."

I smiled as I wrote *Cake And Cookies With Rat Poison* on a yellow legal pad. "Okay, but I'm not paying for a new wardrobe."

After I hung up, I called Alex into my office and filled him in. "Call Charlie DiNapoli and have his friend make another fingerprint setup. Maybe this time we'll get lucky."

CHAPTER THIRTY-ONE

T HE DAY OF RAYMONDO'S EXAMINATION before trial was bright and clear. It began well with a family breakfast at home, a day Sue scheduled for working and bonding with Sylvia. I prepared three cheese omelets, while Sue gave Sylvia her bottle, poured juice for the others, milk for Marcia, and made coffee for the adults.

"Is today pre-school, Marcia?"

"Yes, Daddy."

"What's Miss Gold going to do with you today?"

"We gonna make pictures.

"Of what?"

"Of us."

Seeing my puzzled expression, Sue added: "Each of the children will make drawings of their fellow classmates."

"Wow, you're going to be a portrait artist."

Marcia giggled.

"You like Miss Gold? She a good teacher?"

Marcia nodded vigorously.

"She's terrific," Sue added, " but I'm a little worried."

"I'm glad she's enjoying pre-school, we didn't have it when I was a kid, but what's the problem?"

"I'll fill you in tonight after she's in bed. ... Don't you have to go to the office?" She looked at her watch. "It's ten after nine."

I luxuriated as I ate the last of my omelet and sipped my coffee. "Today's a slow day. I'm examining the driver in the phony accident case. It's scheduled for 10:30. The guy must sleep late."

"Think he'll take the oath?"

"Probably, his lawyer promised, but I wonder if he'll answer any questions."

She poured half cup refills. "I assume you'll make another motion to dismiss which he won't grant. Then I can have more fun in the appellate division. But first I have to put this young lady on the school bus."

"I'll take her on my way out."

AT 10:15, I WALKED INTO the conference room we'd used the last time. "All set?" I asked Alex.

"Yep. And the goodies and special paper are in place."

He pointed to the refreshments table.

"The reporter?"

"On her way. She should be here in a few minutes."

Ten-thirty came and went without the examinee. At eleven, I was about to call when the lawyer and witness arrived. Ayala was immaculately attired, this time in a brown-checked double-breasted suit; Raymondo was in the same jeans and dark, heavy winter jacket he'd worn the last time. I wondered whether they had been washed since then.

"Sorry for the delay, Bill, but Mr. Sanchez's breakfast took longer than I expected. We would have been later if I hadn't reminded him of all the treats you were providing."

Raymondo was already filling two paper plates with cake and cookies. For the next twenty minutes he gorged himself on two platefuls each of butter cookies and Danish pastries, and two containers of coffee heavy on sugar and cream. I began to wonder if a settlement wouldn't be cheaper than feeding the man.

Finally Raymondo looked up. "Okay, let's get this shit over with. I don't have all day."

I turned to the reporter, a dark-haired woman in a sweater and short skirt that showed off a pair of very heavy thighs. "Okay, Consuelo, please swear Mr. Sanchez in."

She did, and he raised his right hand and complied.

"Mr. Sanchez, I'm William Andrews, and I represent the defendant in this case."

Raymondo shrugged. "So?"

"Please state your full name and residence address."

"Raymondo Luis Sanchez, and where I live is none of your fucking business."

I turned to the reporter. "Please mark that for a ruling," then turned back to the witness. "Are you employed?"

"No."

"When were you last employed?"

"Couple of years ago."

"By whom were you employed, and what was the nature of your job?"

"I worked in California." He caught himself. "The rest is none of your fucking business."

"Mark it for a ruling."

Raymondo glared at Bill. "Cut this ruling shit out, and get to the case. My uncle needs the money."

"Then answer my questions so that we can move the case along. What have you been doing to make a living since your last job?"

"Got nothing to do with the case."

The reporter looked up. "Ruling?"

I nodded then looked back at the witness. "Were you involved in an automobile accident on October 15 of last year?"

"Yeah, you know that."

In the next series of questions Raymondo located and

correctly described the section of Washington Heights.

"How many cars were involved in the accident?"

"Two. You know that."

"But *she* doesn't." I pointed to the reporter.

Raymondo shrugged and rose from his seat.

"Where are you going?" I asked, fearing the man was about to skip.

"I'm hungry." Raymondo filled two more plates, refilled his cup and returned to his seat.

"Were you the driver of one of the cars?" Bill asked

"Yeah."

"What was the make, model, and year of the car you were driving?"

"I think it was a Ford."

"You *think* it was a Ford? Don't you know?"

Raymondo shrugged. "I don't remember. It wasn't my car."

"Who's car was it?"

"Don't know. A friend lent it to me."

"What's the name and address of your friend?"

"None of your business."

I turned to the reporter. "Ruling." I reached into my file, took out several sheets of paper, and skimmed them. "According to the police report, you were driving a tan 1997 Ford Fiesta sedan. Is that the car you were operating?"

"I guess. You got the report, why're you asking me?"

"We're here for you to tell us what *you* know."

I removed a few more sheets of paper from the file. "Wasn't it Julio Colon, the manager of South Bronx Auto Sales, who lent you the Ford?"

Raymondo nodded.

"Was that a yes?"

"Yeah."

"And when you brought it back all banged up, Julio was fired?"

"I heard something about that."

"What did you give Julio to lend you the car?"

"Nothing, he was a friend."

"Where is he now?"

"I don't know." He shrugged. "And if I did, I wouldn't tell you."

"Describe the car you hit."

"He hit me, and it's in the police report."

I looked down at my papers. "Was it a Cadillac?"

"Was that what the report said?"

"Just answer the question?"

"What question?"

The reporter read the question back.

"I don't think so. It was one of those foreign cars."

"A blue Honda Accord?"

"Could be."

"How many people were in the car you were driving?"

"Just me and my uncle Juan."

"And how many people were in the Honda you hit?"

Raymondo glared at me. "Stop pulling that shit. He hit me, and it was one drunk guy."

"How'd you know he was drunk?"

Raymondo smiled. "Cause he looked drunk, acted drunk, and smelled drunk."

"That's funny. According to the police report—" I showed him a copy— the man passed the Breathalyzer test with flying colors. How do you explain that?"

Raymondo shrugged. "I guess he paid off the cops."

"The smell—wasn't that because you forced liquor into his mouth and poured some on him?"

"That's a lot of shit," he snapped.

I read the police report again. "According to the police report, there were two witnesses to the accident, Ruben Sanchez, and Carlos Perez. You know them?"

"Yeah, Ruben's a cousin of mine, and Carlos is a friend of the family."

"They weren't in the car with you?"

"Nah, they just happened to be in the neighborhood."

"Raymondo, don't volunteer, just answer his questions," Ayala said.

"You in touch with them?"

"Sometimes."

"You know where they live?"

"Yeah, we gave you their addresses."

"Yes. You gave us three wrong addresses. What are the correct ones?"

"We gave you all you're going to get. Look 'em up in the phone book."

I turned to the reporter, said "ruling," then turned back. "What time did you pick up the car you borrowed from your friend?"

Raymondo scratched his nose. "About seven at night. He was just closing the lot."

"Was your uncle Juan with you when you picked up the car?"

"No, he needed to be driven."

Ayala tapped him on the shoulder. "Just answer the questions, don't volunteer."

Raymondo turned to the lawyer. "Keep your fucking hands off me."

I tensed to keep my face straight. "How come he needed to be driven?"

"He's an old man. He don't walk too good."

"You pick him up with the car you borrowed?"

"Yeah."

"From where did you pick him up?"

Raymondo gave the name and address of a Medicaid nursing home in the South Bronx.

"What time?"

Raymondo looked at his flashy gold-colored watch.

"No, I mean what time did you pick your uncle up?"

"About 7:15."

"Where'd you take him?"

"Out for dinner."

"Where?"

"Santiago's. It's a Spanish restaurant in Washington Heights near where your guy ran into us."

"What did you have to eat?"

"I don't remember, but it was good."

"Who paid for it?"

"Uncle Juan."

"You have the credit card slip?"

"No, he paid cash."

"What did you have to drink?"

"My uncle had a beer, and I had Coke. Not like your drunken bum."

"Stop volunteering. Just answer the questions," said Ayala.

Raymondo shrugged.

"Before the accident, how long had your uncle been in the nursing home?"

The man rubbed his forehead. "Maybe a couple of years."

"And how often had you visited him?"

"When I was in town."

"What was the date of the last time you visited him before the date of the accident."

He glared at me. "What's this have to do with the case?"

I glared back. "Because it proves that you only visited your uncle to drive him to the phony accident."

Raymondo rose and pulled back his fist. When I stared calmly back, the man turned, filled his pockets from the refreshment table, and stomped out of the room.

I turned to the reporter. "This examination is adjourned pending rulings."

"No, it's not," said Ayala. "It's over, you've had all you're entitled to."

"Okay, Alex," I said, "prepare the motion."

THAT EVENING AFTER DINNER, we were sipping coffee in the living room. I was just going to ask about Marcia's preschool problem when Sue jumped in ahead. "Anything new on your quest for a more interesting but less profitable law practice?"

I wondered whether this was genuine interest or a ploy to put off the other problem, but I went along. "Matter of fact there is. Harvey told me about an organization called *Death Penalty Information Center* in Washington D.C. I wrote away to them and I'm waiting to hear."

She frowned. "Death penalty cases—sounds very time-consuming."

"Probably is, but it could give the firm good publicity." She shrugged, and I decided to get back to our daughter.

"What's bothering you about Marcia's pre-school?" I asked.

She knit her brow. "It's probably nothing, but I think Miss Gold is too easy on her."

"How so?"

She went to the den, returned with a thin folder, and handed it to me.

There were six sheets of paper, each with a stamped date, and all covered with scribbling. "What's this?"

"Marcia's three art classes. I spoke to Miss Gold and she said that some children pick up art more slowly."

I shook my head. "Hey, give her some breathing room. Don't do to her what my father did to me," referring to my very demanding father who controlled me from the grave for many years.

She nodded. "Maybe you're right, but I'm a little worried."

I got up and hugged her, but hoped she was wrong.

CHAPTER THIRTY-TWO

LESS THAN TWO WEEKS LATER, I served and filed the disclosure motion, and made sure I'd be in court. As always, Robbins called the lawyers into his robing room—but there the similarity ended. He leaned his elbow on the desk, chin resting on his palm, and stared at me. "Andrews, I'm getting sick and tired of being subjected to those disclosure and discovery motions."

Here we go again, I thought. "There's an easy way of ending them," I replied.

"Really?"

"Recuse yourself from the case, and let me bother your successor."

The judge chuckled. "You'd like that. I'll bet you think you'll get one of my colleagues who's in your insurance company's pocket."

I shook my head. "Just someone who'll be fair to both sides."

The judge's frown slowly turned to a faint smile. "No, I have a better idea."

He pressed the intercom button.

"Have Mrs. Chan come in and see me. . . . Yes, *now*."

We waited in stony silence for nearly ten minutes until there was a light knock on the door. "Come in, Thelma."

A thin Asian woman in a plain-gray skirt-suit came in, looked around the room and asked hesitantly, "you wanted to see me, Judge?"

"Yes. Gentlemen, as I'm sure you know, Mrs. Chan, my law secretary." He moved his finger past the three of us. "And *these* are the eminent counsel in the Ramos case."

She nodded. "I've met them."

"For a period of well over a year, I've been subjected to the excessive demands for discovery and disclosure by this man." He pointed to me. "These games have so far bought the insurance company too much time, and they have kept the plaintiff from being compensated for his injuries. I am sick and tired of this nonsense, and I am leaving the discovery and disclosure aspects of this case in your capable hands." He handed the file to her. "Thelma, take these gentlemen with you and resolve this motion—subject, of course, to my review."

"Gentlemen, please follow me." We went into the courtroom, which, except for the clerk and court officer, was empty. She led us into chambers, a small suite to the immediate left, the two sets of rooms having originally been a single impressive courtroom. Chambers consisted of a small reception area with a secretarial desk and three adjoining rooms. A plump African American woman was inputting into a keyboard. "Ellen, is the conference room available for a meeting?"

"You're in luck, dear. I cleared out the judge's mess from the table this morning."

Thelma nodded and led us into a twelve-by-ten-foot room with bookshelves covering the far wall, and a small, scratched wooden table with six chairs. She motioned us to be seated, skimmed the file, set up a chart on a legal pad, and looked up. "Okay, before Mr. Sanchez walked out of his examination, there were five questions Mr. Andrews marked for a ruling. He set them out in his motion papers and numbered them, which makes this easy. I have to rule on the five refused questions, on whether Mr. Sanchez will have to come back and complete his examination, and whether Mr. Ayala will be allowed to restore the case to the trial calendar. Anything I've missed?"

"Sounds complete to me," I said.

Ayala nodded.

"Now I'll hear argument, item by item, starting with the

five rulings." She turned to Ayala. "Your witness gave his name, but refused to give his residence address. Why is that?"

"Where he lives has nothing to do with the accident."

"What do you say to that, Mr. Andrews?" she asked keeping a straight face.

"As you know, Ms. Chan, we believe this was a staged accident, and the man is lying through his teeth. We need to make a thorough investigation to learn more about him and see whether we can discredit him at trial. His correct address is step number one in the process."

"Didn't you get his address from the police report?"

"No, the addresses in the police report of all three witnesses were fictitious. The address Mr. Sanchez gave was an empty lot. The address one of the other witnesses gave was a *bodega*."

"What do you say to that?" she asked turning back to Ayala.

"We're not obligated to do investigations for the insurance company."

"Okay, let's get on to question number two," she said with a straight face.

For the next forty-five minutes we presented our arguments, and she listened patiently, asked several incisive questions, and made notes on her chart. When all seven items had been separately argued, she looked up. "Okay, I'll prepare a decision, run it by the judge, and send the final result to both of you. It will provide for an order to be settled on notice. Thank you for your attention. Have a good day."

As we left the chambers, Ayala turned to me. "She's a lot easier to deal with than her boss."

"I just hope he lets *her* make the decisions."

AT 5:00 P.M. A FEW DAYS LATER, Thelma Chan was leaving to go home and rescue her mother-in-law from the tender mercy of her twin sons. The older woman had been caring for her grandsons while their regular nanny was recovering from a bad cold. As she reached the door to chambers, Thelma was startled by a shout coming from the judge's office. "Thelma, come in here!"

She found Robbins seated behind his desk, his face flushed. "Yes, Judge."

"Did you write this?" he demanded, waving a sheaf of papers in front of him.

She took them and, after a brief look, placed them on the desk. "That's the Ramos decision you assigned to me."

"You gave the crooked tennis player everything he asked for. I didn't tell you to do that."

She clamped her hands on her hips and stared into his eyes. "You told me to resolve the motion. I had a hearing, heard arguments, and concluded that the defendant was fully entitled to everything he asked for. You can, of course, deny the motion, in which event the defendant will most likely appeal, get another reversal, and start us on our journey back to the civil court. Do whatever you please—I'm going home to my family." She turned on her heels and left.

CHAPTER THIRTY-THREE

O MY SURPRISE, THE DECISION GAVE ME nearly everything I asked for. The only things the judge had done to his law secretary's decision was to extend the compliance time from one month to two, and eliminate a threatened dismissal for non-compliance. After the order was signed, I arranged with Ayala for the resumed examination date which he wanted to be near the end of the two month period. As he explained to me, it took time to contact his witness.

When the stipulation fixing the date and time was signed, I called Charlie with the date. "Think we need Joe Regan's dog-and-pony show?" I asked him, just to be on the safe side.

"I doubt it, but I'll ask him."

AT 6:00 IN THE EVENING A FEW DAYS LATER, my intercom buzzed. "Hi, Gordon—what's up?"

"I have a visitor who knows you. We're about to open a bottle of twelve-year-old Dewars. Please join us."

"Be my pleasure," I replied, my mouth watering. "I won't even ask who it is."

When I entered my partner's equally messy office, Gordon was seated behind his curved desk, glass in hand. A small portion on the left had been cleared of papers and contained a scotch bottle, an ice bucket, and an empty glass. The third glass was just being carried to the lips of Joe Regan.

I shook his hand. "*Joe!* How the hell are you? I didn't know you two knew each other."

"Joe and I go back a long way," Jones said. "He's a great investigator. I've been using him ever since he retired from the force."

"Yeah," Regan added. "We're first cousins. Grew up together."

I pointed to the bottle.

"Of course, and for us, too."

I filled all three glasses with ice and scotch, took a sip, and continued, "I didn't know you were an Irishman, Gordon."

"About an eighth—my best part. This guy—" he added, pointing to Regan, "is a half."

"I guess us Jewish Protestants had better watch our steps."

"You're a nice guy," Joe answered. "We'll let you in the club."

For a while, we just enjoyed the scotch. Then Joe spoke up. "I really came to see you Bill, but I ran into him in the lobby, and I'd never turn down free twelve-year-old scotch. Charlie called me yesterday and told me what you asked. He's right that you don't need me for the follow-up exam of the clown, even though I do like your money."

I smiled, thinking this is a guy I can trust. "That's only insurance company money. You'll get mine when I start using you for my plaintiff's cases. I assume that DNA won't be available."

Joe sipped his drink. "I don't think so. We couldn't find anything usable the first two times, and we looked real hard—but there's a worse problem."

Bill stared at him.

"The guy's fingerprints didn't show up in our California search."

Bill frowned. "Why only California? Maybe he lied about where he last worked."

"The national data base is FBI, and they've tightened up. They're insisting on an actual criminal case or investigation before they let state police use it."

"Damn!" My lips tightened. "Could you check New

York and Puerto Rico?"

"We did. There's nothing. I think you ought to push hard on past employment."

"I guess I'll have to, but Sanchez doesn't say much."

RAYMONDO'S EXAMINATION WAS SCHEDULED for 10:00 A.M. fifteen days later. Ayala had suggested the earlier hour and promised to be on time. Amazingly they arrived five minutes early. The lawyer, as usual, was dressed to the nines. This time it was a tan glen-plaid. Raymondo wore his usual outfit, and I wondered if that was all he owned. By ten-twenty-five he had wolfed down three platefuls before he indicated he was ready to testify.

"Good morning Mr. Sanchez," I began.

Raymondo stuffed a Danish into his mouth and chewed noisily.

I smiled. "Mr. Sanchez, this is a continuation of your examination before trial, being held pursuant to court order. Do you understand you are still under oath?"

Raymondo shrugged.

"Please answer the question. Do you understand you are still under oath? Say yes or no."

"Yes or no?"

Ayala whispered into his ear.

The man studied his lawyer before he turned to me. "Yeah, I understand."

"Okay, let's start with the questions the court ordered you to answer. Please state your full name and residence address."

"My name is Raymondo Luis Sanchez, and I live around."

"What does that mean, that you live around?"

"I don't live in a fixed place. I travel around and stay with friends and family."

"What address does your mail come to?"

"I don't get any."

"Are you a U.S. citizen?"

"*Sure.*"

"At what address are you registered to vote?"

"I don't vote."

"What address do you put on your tax returns?"

Sanchez was about to give the expected answer when Ayala waved his hand in front of the witness's face. "Don't answer that. Mr. Sanchez refuses to answer on the ground that it may tend to incriminate him."

"When did you last *have* a residence address?"

Sanchez scrunched his brow and appeared to think. "About five years ago."

"Where was that?"

"In Frisco."

"That's San Francisco?

"Yeah."

"Was there more than on place you lived in San Francisco?"

"No, only one."

"What was that address?"

Sanchez shrugged. "I don't remember."

"Did you live anywhere in California other than San Francisco?"

"No, just there. . . . Can't you hurry this up? I don't have all day."

I felt ready to explode, but kept my cool. "Sorry, Mr. Sanchez, but I need a lot of information from you. . . . When you lived in San Francisco, were you working?"

"Yeah."

"What was the name and address of your employer?"

"I don't remember. I was selling cars in a used car lot."

"Were you working on the books—that is, was withholding tax being taken out of your pay?"

At that point Ayala spoke up. "Look, he'll check his records and memory and insert whatever information his has about his employment in San Francisco."

"Including name and address of employer, dates of employment, et cetera.?"

"Yeah, whatever he has or can remember."

I turned to the reporter. "Leave a big space in the transcript." I looked at an outline on my legal pad. "Who is Ruben Sanchez?"

"He was one of the witnesses who saw your guy crash into the back of my car."

"So you claim he was a witness to the crash?"

"Yeah."

"He related to you?"

"Yeah, a cousin. His mother was my aunt."

"So he's a first cousin."

Raymondo shrugged, and Ayala nodded.

"What is Ruben's correct, current residence address?"

"I told—"

"Ayala held up his hand. "We'll insert that in the transcript when Mr. Sanchez signs it."

I nodded to the reporter. "Who is Carlos Perez?"

"He's a friend of the family and Ruben's closest buddy."

"And you claim he was a witness to the crash?"

"Yeah."

"What is—"

Ayala cut in. "We will supply Mr. Perez's correct, current residence address when Mr. Sanchez signs the transcript."

I told the reporter to leave a space. "Mr. Sanchez you've previously testified that you and your uncle had dinner together at a Spanish restaurant right before the car crash that's the subject of this case. Was anyone else having dinner with you?"

"No, just me and Uncle Juan."

"Weren't Ruben and Carlos in the restaurant with you?"

"Nah I didn't see them?"

"How big was the restaurant?"

"It was small, maybe ten or twelve tables."

The examination dragged on for a day and a half. I pulled out a substantial amount of information, including the fact that Raymondo had also worked in Washington State. While I didn't get everything I wanted, I decided it was enough from Sanchez. I could get more from the plaintiff and the other two witnesses.

CHAPTER THIRTY-FOUR

WHILE I WAS WAITING FOR THE INFORMATION to get into the transcript of Raymondo's examination, I had Alex prepare and serve the notice for plaintiff's examination. I was met with a motion for a protective order on the grounds that the judge had granted one when I originally noticed the plaintiff.

When I pointed out that the protective order had been reversed by the appellate division, Ayala replied that his client was too sick to be examined.

At the call of the motion calender, we were back in the robing room. As we took seats, the judge fastened his eyes on me. "Another frivolous motion?"

"Yes, Your Honor," I replied, "But the motion is by Mr. Ayala, and I do agree that it's frivolous."

Robbins smiled broadly. "Then I can penalize you for frivolous opposition."

"There's no reason at all for you to bother yourself with it," I said, wondering whether the judge ever kept his word.

"The last time we were here, you assigned all of our discovery and disclosure motions to Ms. Chan."

". . .You trying to tell me how to run *my* court?" he growled.

"No, I'm just reminding you of what you said."

Robbins let out a breath. "Oh, well, it'll be good to get rid of you." He pressed the intercom.

A half hour later we were again seated around the tiny conference table in the judge's chambers. This time, though, the law secretary had to clear off several days of luncheon detritus. She looked up from the motion papers into Ayala's eyes. "Why does this have to be a motion? You knew that the original protective order had been reversed by the appellate division."

Ayala, unused to being on the receiving end, was flustered. "I-I had to protect my client."

She stared fixedly at him.

"Mr. Ramos is in a nursing home and too sick to come to his office." Ayala pointed at me.

"So we'll hold it at the nursing home. All you had to do was ask. A phone call is a lot easier than a motion—or were you just trying to run up an expense for the insurance company?"

"You'd never give me anything without a court order."

"*Bull!*" I exclaimed.

"Okay," she said, taking charge. "Unfortunately, this *is* a motion. You'll get a decision shortly," she concluded shooing us out.

A week went by before a decision denying the motion came, directing the plaintiff to be examined at the nursing home, and giving me my entire shopping list, except for a frivolous motion penalty that I knew couldn't possibly be in my cards from the Robbins deck.

I immediately sent out a notice and had Alex order a reporter. Since we knew the plaintiff claimed to speak only Spanish, I also had Alex order an interpreter.

THE FOUR-STORY SOUTH BRONX LONG-TERM Care Center at the corner of 150th Street and Jerome Avenue had a grim gray exterior, matched by the chilly overcast weather. As we crossed the entrance hall, our nostrils were offended by the odor of stale urine partially masked by an unpleasantly strong disinfectant. I rang a bell on the reception desk, and waited for several minutes until the receptionist waddled back to her station. On being told the purpose of our visit, the near-three-hundred-pound, five-foot woman told us we would be using the conference room on the third floor, and that she had sent several people up there already.

In the ten-by-twelve-foot freshly painted white walled room, furnished with a faux-walnut-topped table and ten chairs, we found Consuelo, the reporter who had covered Raymondo's examination, and a short, thin man, with thick wire-rimmed glasses who introduced himself as Alberto Martinez, the Spanish interpreter.

I was about to use the phone to locate Ayala and his client when the impeccably dressed lawyer arrived followed by the plaintiff, a small roly-poly man with fat cheeks. He was wearing a hospital gown, and seated in a wheelchair pushed by an orderly.

At the lawyer's direction the chair was moved to the far end of the table and the orderly left. Ayala seated himself next to his client, removed a file from a tan leather briefcase, and placed it on the table. "I assume you are the interpreter," he said to Martinez.

"Alberto Martinez. My card," he said. handing one each to Ayala and me.

"I trust you're competent, because I am fluent in Spanish and will know if you're not."

The little man knit his brow. "Perhaps you would like to give me a test, señor?"

Ayala shook his head. "No need, let's get on with this."

"Consuelo," I said, "please give Mr. Martinez his oath."

The reporter swore in the interpreter and then the witness.

After identifying him, I asked for the details of the accident, which the man answered identically to the affidavit he had signed earlier.

When I asked about his injuries, he said that he was only eighty-one and before the accident could get around with a walker, but that he was now limited to a wheelchair.

I shifted to the three witnesses. Raymondo and Ruben were nephews, sons of his sisters; Carlos was a friend of the family. "Mr. Ramos, how long have you been living in this nursing home?"

"About four or five years. I came here after my wife died."

"Is this the first nursing home you've been in?"

He nodded.

"Please answer in words."

"Yes, it is."

"Do you get many visitors?"

"The only one who visited me here was Raymondo."

"How often has *he* visited you here?"

The man puffed out his cheeks as he thought. "Maybe two or three times."

"When did he last visit you before the day of the accident?"

"...About a year or two before. He told me his mother had just died."

"Had he ever taken you out of the nursing home before

the day of the accident?"

"No that was the first time."

I noticed that Ayala was looking uncomfortable. "How come he took you out then?"

"He said he thought I'd like to have dinner out, and it seemed like a good idea to me."

"Where did he take you to eat?"

"It was a Spanish restaurant—I think in Manhattan. I don't remember the name."

"Was it good?"

Ramos shrugged. "It was okay. I've had better—especially at home."

"What did you eat?"

"I had *paella*."

"What kind?"

"*Marinera*—you know, the kind with only seafood, no chicken or sausage."

"What about Raymondo? What did he have?"

"*Mariscada* with shrimp and scallops. He had two portions. He's a big eater, and I was paying." The little man snickered.

"I know, I've seen him eat. What about Ruben and Carlos? What did they have?"

"*Paella*, same as me."

At that juncture Ayala started talking to his client in Spanish.

"Stop coaching him," I demanded, then, turning to Martinez, "translate what he said so the reporter can take it down."

"Raymondo told me only you and he ate dinner that day," the interpreter said.

"But he made a mistake. He didn't understand."

"If he made a mistake, you can correct it by examining him after I finish or have him submit a corrective affidavit when he signs the transcript."

Ayala shrugged but said nothing further, and after I had finished questioning Ramos, he wisely declined to cross examine his client.

As I left the nursing home, I wondered what the signed transcript would look like. I doubted that Miguel would follow the rules. It wasn't in his nature.

CHAPTER THIRTY-FIVE

Y PREMONITION ABOUT THE RAMOS TRANSCRIPT wasn't confirmed for nearly four months. I'd sent it to Ayala for signature three weeks after the examination, and had sent him Raymondo's nearly two months before that. A month after the Ramos transcript went out, I'd made several calls to give the man a gentle nudge. After three of mine I'd finally gotten a return call. "What the hell are you bothering me for, Andrews?"

"I thought you wanted to move this case."

"I do but you won't let me."

"If you'd give me what I'm entitled to, you could get the case on the calendar."

"I've given you Ramos and Sanchez. What more do you want?"

I picked up a marking pen and printed *B U L L* in large block letters on a yellow legal pad. "How about filled-in, signed, and notarized transcripts, and an examination of your other two witnesses?"

". . .Okay," the other snapped. I'll talk to my people and try to push them."

ANOTHER MONTH, WITH FIVE MORE unreturned phone calls, passed without result. I wrote a demand letter threatening a motion. This too was ignored, and Alex prepared the motion. Just before it was served, Alex walked into my office with a large envelope bearing Ayala's name and return address. "Look what Santa sent us, and it's not even Christmas."

"What's in it?"

"I assume the transcripts. I thought you'd want to open it."

"No, you can have that honor. Copy it, give me a set, and we can talk about it later."

That afternoon a certified letter went to Ayala returning the transcripts as completely unsatisfactory. Raymondo's transcript was signed but not notarized, and none of the agreed upon information was inserted. The Ramos one was signed and notarized, but the answer to the question: *What about Ruben and Carlos? What did they have?* was crossed out with a black marker, and the following language was written in: *They weren't there. I didn't see them any time that day or evening.*

Alex sent Ayala a certified letter detailing the problem and warning that, if the deficiencies were not corrected within two weeks, an appropriate motion would be made.

When he got it, Ayala phoned his forwarding attorney and was told by Maria that her boss was away on vacation.

We filed the motion. The answering papers were sketchy at best, concluding that the defendant's attorneys had received all they were entitled to and accusing us of improper delaying tactics. On the call of the calendar both attorneys answered ready, expecting a trip to the robing room followed by a meeting with the law secretary, but Robbins short-cut the process. "Referred to Ms. Chan—Thelma, take them away."

At the courtroom door, the law secretary turned to her charges. "Our conference room is in the process of updating our lighting. Judge McKenna is allowing us to use his." She led us to the Administrative Judge's chambers. We entered a room nearly twice the size of Robbins's tiny one. It had a highly polished dark-wood table, twelve leather chairs, and both long walls were lined with book shelves. Thelma motioned us to seats then seated herself directly opposite Ayala. In a quiet nearly kindly tone she raked him over the coals. "Mr. Ayala, if the dean of your law school saw what you've done, he'd take back your degree. How dare you send out such garbage? You're supposed to be an experienced trial attorney. Do you have an excuse?"

"Mr. Sanchez is very difficult to deal with. I sent Mr. Andrews what I had. It took many calls from my forwarding attorney just to get him to sign and mail it."

"That's no excuse," she replied, looking him in the eyes. "He promised some information, and he must keep his promises. And what about the other two witnesses? Can't you produce them for Mr. Andrews?"

"I'll do my best to get them," Ayala answered, flustered.

"And what about plaintiff's examination? What possessed you to cross out and interliniate the transcript?"

"Mr. Andrews confused my client. The other two witnesses weren't in the restaurant. The change had to be made to tell the truth."

The law secretary screwed up her face. "That's not the way to do it. You know the rules. . . . My decision will require you to make all the required insertions, do all corrections properly, and produce the other two witnesses within thirty days or prohibit the testimony of your client and the three witnesses. I suspect Judge Robbins will give you more time and leave out the penalties." She turned to me and, with a twinkle in her eye, she added, "I suspect he has something against crooked tennis players. You might consider taking up golf."

CHAPTER THIRTY-SIX

ROUND THE SAME TIME, Charlie DiNapoli found a memo on his desk from a fellow investigator named Dick Wilson. *See me on Ramos.* The memo was dated the day before. Charlie called Wilson's cell phone and got his voice mail. "Got your memo on Ramos. What's up? Call me."

An hour later, Charlie was inputting memos into his computer with one finger, using the other hand to drink coffee, when his cell phone buzzed. "Hi, Charlie, Dick said. Remember Concetta, the waitress from the catering place?"

"Yeah, I asked you to interview her."

"She kept ducking me. Anyway, I got a call from her yesterday. She wants to meet. I figured that, since Ramos is yours, you'd want to talk to her. Her number's on my desk pad."

Charlie left a message for her which she returned the next day. He arranged to meet her at a Starbucks on Broadway, a few blocks from the hotel, the next morning before she went to work.

SHE WAS SEATED AT A SMALL TABLE away from the service counter, and he ordered two coffees and a Danish. "What happened to you?" he asked as he set the order down. The long dark wavy hair, and the near pretty face with slightly puffy cheeks, was the same as before, but the black-and-blue marks around her left eye were new.

She added sugar and cream to her coffee and took a sip. "My cheating boyfriend didn't like it when I threw him out of my apartment. That's what I wanted to talk to you about."

"Oh?" He took a sip of his coffee.

She bit into the pastry. "You're a cop?"

"I used to be. Now I'm an insurance investigator."

She picked up her cup, then put it down again. "It's about that three-million-dollar policy that one of the guys at the club has? I think his name is Berger?"

Charlie nodded. "That's one of the cases I have."

"I told my boyfriend about it." She chewed her pastry slowly. "I understand he had an accident."

"It was no accident."

"I heard there's a lawsuit, and my boyfriend's gonna get a piece of it."

Charlie pulled a spiral notebook from an inside pocket, and looked at a page. "Your boy friend is Julio Sanchez?"

"Was."

"What did he have to do with the accident?"

"He gave my information to a guy he was in prison with, and he was promised a piece of the action."

"What's the guy's name?"

She scrunched up her brow. "I . . . Oh, yeah, same name. He thought it was funny to share a cell with another Sanchez."

"Raymondo Sanchez?"

"I think so."

"Where was he in prison?"

"He told me somewhere in New Mexico."

That was all the information she had. He asked her to sign a statement, and she said she'd think about it, but she seemed hesitant. He left the Starbucks wondering where he could get a New Mexico contact.

CHAPTER
THIRTY-SEVEN

THE DECISION WAS JUST AS the law secretary had predicted. Ayala promptly complied with the part concerning the Ramos transcript. His affidavit stated what he'd meant to say was: "They weren't there. I didn't see them any time that day. Someone must have told me what Ruben and Carlos ate that evening." I had a good laugh when I read it.

Raymondo's situation was a different story. The two months passed with nothing forthcoming. My phone calls and letters evoked no response. I was about to have Alex prepare another motion when Raymondo's transcript came. It had been notarized, and all the agreed-upon information had been responded to. There was only one problem: The addresses filled in for Ruben Sanchez and Carlos Perez were the same wrong ones from the police report and discovery answers.

This time Ayala returned my call promptly. "You called me about the addresses Sanchez gave for the other two witnesses?"

"Right on!" I replied.

"I noticed it too and yelled at the man."

"I'll bet I can give you his answer. He told you I could ask for them at the trial."

Ayala laughed. "You' been meeting with my witness on the sly? Tell you what, let me try to push him to produce his buddies for examination."

The plan succeeded; two weeks later, the dates and times for the examination of the two witnesses had been agreed upon. They were scheduled for the bugged conference room Joe Regan was monitoring.

ON THE DAY OF THE EXAMINATIONS, Ayala and the two witnesses arrived promptly at 9:30. The two men were extreme contrasts in both appearance and attitude. Ruben Sanchez was a short, wiry, taciturn man; Carlos Perez was over six feet tall with a protruding belly and a talkative manner. Their only similarity were that both wore jeans and loud Hawaiian shirts.

I started with Sanchez while Perez waited in another room and stuffed himself with cake and coffee. Ruben

Sanchez was the kind of witness every litigator wanted to present to opposing counsel. He gave short, precise answers and volunteered nothing. He told his story, and said that he and his friend had been at a movie and hadn't known his uncle and cousin would be eating in the same neighborhood. He'd eaten dinner at home before he went to the movies, had never been convicted of a crime, and didn't believe either Raymondo or Carlos had. When asked where he lived, he suppled a plausible Bronx address. I got no value from him except for a fingerprint on his water cup.

While Ruben Sanchez was, from Ayala's standpoint, a dream witness, Carlos Perez was a nightmare. The man's mouth was constantly open either taking in food and drink or answering unasked questions. My first question was the man's address. After giving it he continued, "I guess you want to hear about the old man's accident. The car was stopped when—"

Ayala held up his hand, "Carlos, wait until he asks you a question. Don't volunteer."

"Oh, sure. Like I was saying, the car was—"

The examination went on in that vein for a long while. The man told his story about going to the movies, and unasked, gave most of the movie plot, which I'd assumed he'd seen on a different occasion. He too said he had no prior convictions and launched into a long story about what an honest man he was. Perez had met Juan Ramos only once, several years before.

After nearly two hours, I recognized that I was getting nowhere and said, "Carlos, I guess you enjoyed the picture?"

"Yeah, it was great. One of the best."

"You have supper before?"

"I sure did. No fun seeing a show on an empty stomach."

"I bet I know what you had?"

"Yeah?" he replied with a laugh.

"*Paella marinara*?"

"How'd you know?"

"You look like a *paella* guy. Was it good?"

"Not bad."

"How much did it cost?"

"How the fuck would I know? The old man was paying."

Ayalaa started screaming objections as the examination concluded.

When they left the conference room, I wondered how Carlos's fairy tale would read. I also wondered how Ayala could possibly believe the crap his witnesses were spouting.

CHAPTER
THIRTY-EIGHT

THE SIGNED TRANSCRIPTS CAME BACK promptly. Carlos's included an affidavit stating that what he had meant to say was: "My father bought us dinner."

The transcripts were accompanied by a motion asking that the case be restored to the trial calendar in the same place it had been when it was removed by the appellate division. In checking the law journal, I learned that granting the motion would mean a trial date within the next two or three months. I opposed the motion and cross-moved for more disclosure on the basis that Carlos's affidavit was proof of my need.

In court the judge immediately referred us to his law secretary. "Please be seated, gentlemen," she said when we entered the conference room. "We've cleaned up the table for you." She pointed to the pristine surface.

I was enjoying her subtle humor, and replied in kind. "We're most appreciative, Ms. Chan. The sheen is near dazzling."

She chuckled. "Now that we've completed the fictional part of this visit, let's get down to the case." She removed a finger's length of papers from the court file jacket. "Since I assumed Judge Robbins would refer the motion to me, I read all of your papers with great care, and I think I understand your positions."

Ayala frowned. "Does that mean you won't hear argument?"

"No. If either of you wants to argue, I'll hear it, but first let me tell you how I see this motion."

She took off her glasses, wiped her eyes with a tissue, replaced them, and looked down at the papers. "First, as Mr. Ayala correctly points out, the case has grown long in the tooth. Mr. Andrews responds that the delays were not caused by the defendant but by the plaintiff's witnesses, which was countenanced by the court and reversed by the appellate division, which also removed the case from the trial calendar. Nonetheless, the plaintiff is an old man entitled to a day in court during his lifetime."

"What about the Perez transcript?" I interjected, leaning forward in my seat.

She held up a hand. "Patience, Mr. Andrews, I was just getting to that. The claimed misstatement by Mr. Perez that 'The old man was paying' creates a strong impression that the plaintiff and the three witnesses had dinner together before the accident and supports the defendant's belief that they were brought along to witness a staged accident. Mr. Andrews is certainly entitled to a resumed examination of Perez and his father, and to make investigations indicated by the recent examinations. So what I think I'm going to do, subject to the judge's final say, is order Mr. Perez's continued examination and his father's examination within thirty days, and to place the case back on the trial calendar in its original position."

"But that doesn't give me enough time before the trial date to do *anything*," I nearly shouted.

She again lifted her hand and pushed the palm towards me.

"Calm down Mr. Andrews, there's more. The order should also provide for the defendant's right to continued disclosure and discovery, and, since Judge Robbins intends to try the case, the defendant should have the right to at least six months of trial adjournments for continued disclosure and discovery."

"Okay by me," replied Ayala.

I nodded. "I can live with it—*if* the numbers stay the same and he doesn't drag his feet."

"I'll do the best I can, but my witnesses are funny peo-ple," Ayala said.

WHEN WE GOT BACK TO THE OFFICE, Alex followed me into my room. "Something puzzling you?" I asked noticing the expression on the young man's face.

"Yeah, who won that one?"

I chuckled. My young associate was becoming more perceptive. "Good question. I think they did. She gave us Perez and his father, which we're absolutely entitled to, but Ayala gets a trial in two or three months after dragging his feet on our disclosure and discovery for over two years."

"What about the six months?"

I shook my head. "That's window dressing. We won't get half that without proving to Robbins exactly what we're looking to find, which gives Ayala the power to throw an-other monkey wrench into the works."

CHAPTER THIRTY-NINE

THE DECISION CAME DOWN just as the law secretary had said it would, with no downward revisions by Judge Robbins. I reached out to Charlie DiNapoli for an update. I'd been selecting a jury in a heavy plaintiff's case in federal court, that I'd hoped would get me some good referrals, so the meeting was held in the early evening at my office.

Since I'd been out for several days, my secretary had taken the opportunity to undo some of my mess, and my papers were sorted in neat piles along both sides of my rectangular desk, with the center clear. It looked good, and I wondered whether I could keep it that way. Alex and I were in shirt sleeves sipping coffee when Charlie arrived. "Smells good," he said as he unzipped his jacket and took a seat next to Alex.

I shook my visitor's hand then turned to my associate. "Alex, get our friend a cup."

"How do you take it, Charlie?"

"Straight black, thanks."

Alex filled a mug from a steaming carafe, placed it in front of Charlie, and resumed his seat.

The investigator took a sip, opened the folder he'd brought, and pulled out a sheet. "As you know, I wasn't getting much for quite a while—what you got from Sanchez and the other two clowns went practically nowhere, but I ran into something a few weeks ago that looks promising. Remember the waitress in the hotel I told you about?"

"Concetta? I thought she was ducking you."

"She was, but I got lucky." He told me about his meeting with her.

"Were you able to follow it up in New Mexico?"

"Sort of."

"Sort of?"

Charlie took a sip of coffee. "Yeah. I reached out to the New Mexico Corrections Department, explained my problem to one of their people, and sent him a copy of the fingerprint.

The fingerprint matched Julio Sanchez's cell-mate, but it wasn't Raymondo. The guy's name was Ralph Lawrence Santo. The man got out on parole a few years ago and skipped. His parole officer would like to find him."

My face lit up. "Maybe we can help him. I'm sure Jerry will pay his way to New York. You did a great job."

"There's more." Charlie pulled another sheet from his folder. "This is still preliminary. You asked about Carlos Perez's father."

I nodded.

"We checked the address he gave, and he lives there."

I chuckled. "In this case, that's unusual."

"Sure is. He lives with his mother and kid sister."

"What about the father?"

"So far we haven't found him, but one of our investigators is asking around the neighborhood."

I drained my mug. "Maybe your luck will hold."

A MONTH AFTER THE ORDER WAS SIGNED, Ayala called. "I can get you Perez two weeks from Wednesday."

I glanced at my diary. "Looks good. I'll send you a notice. What's his father's name? We might as well get both of them at the same sitting."

"What you need him for?" Ayala replied, annoyed.

"For the same reason you wrote that bullshit affidavit."

"I had to do *something*."

"Why don't you try the truth? . . . Still better, why don't you get a case you can make some money on?"

"Look, I asked the kid for his father, but I couldn't get

an answer. Why don't you ask him when you examine?"

When he hung up, I called Charlie and asked him to push the search for Carlos's father.

CARLOS PEREZ'S CONTINUED EXAMINATION was held in the same conference room as his original one. Since we already had his fingerprints, I saved Jerry Arthur some money and didn't call on Joe Regan. Ayala and the witness arrived promptly at 9:30, and like Raymondo, Carlos first attacked the refreshments. Twenty minutes later, I started. "Mr. Perez, I remind you that you are still under oath."

Carlos shrugged. "Yeah, I know, but this time no fucking tricks."

I put on a stern expression. "What tricks?"

"You asked me how much my dinner cost."

"That's a legitimate question, and you said you didn't know because 'the old man paid for it.'"

"Yeah, but the old man was my father, not Ramos."

"What's your father's name?"

"Jaime—Jaime Perez."

"You live with him?"

"No. He and my mom split about ten years ago."

"Where does he live?"

"In Puerto Rico." Carlos reached into his pocket, pulled out an address book, and gave an address in San Juan.

"Where did you and your father have dinner on the

night of the accident?"

"He wasn't there."

I suppressed a smile with a frown. "If he wasn't there, how did he pay for your dinner?"

"That's easy. He sent me a hundred dollar pre-paid Visa card for my birthday. I used that."

"Where did you have dinner that night?"

"At Fernandez's. It's a Spanish diner in my neighborhood."

"Then the price of the dinner would be on the Visa slip you signed?"

"I guess so, but I threw it away."

"What's the Visa card number?"

"I don't know. I used up the hundred bucks and threw it away."

"So you and Ruben had dinner on your father that night?"

"Yeah—"

Ayala spoke to the witness in rapid Spanish.

"I mean no. Ruben ate home."

"Mr. Ayala!" I shouted. *"Stop coaching the witness!* What did you say to him?"

"None of your business," the lawyer replied with a smirk. "You were trying to trick him, and I just reminded him to be accurate."

I turned back to Perez. "Your last answer was what

your lawyer told you to say. Wasn't it?"

"No, I just made a mistake. He wasn't with me at dinner."

"Who was?"

". . . My sister Rosa."

"Just her?"

"Yeah."

"She live with you?"

"Used to. She got married and moved to California. She's now Rosa Diaz." He pulled out the address book and gave his sister's address.

"You planning to examine the father and the sister?" Ayala growled.

"Could be," I replied. "Maybe *someone* will tell the truth."

The examination concluded shortly thereafter, and I called Charlie with the names and addresses of two more witnesses to be interviewed.

CHAPTER FORTY

ON SUNDAY MORNING THREE WEEKS LATER, the senior members of the Andrews family were trying to sleep late, but we should have known that was not to be. It was the nanny's weekend off, and we were alone with our two children. Promptly at seven-thirty the bedroom door opened and a five-year-old girl began shaking her father. "Daddy, Sylvia and I are hungry. We want breakfast."

This awakened their mother, who sat up. "Marcia, didn't you forget something?"

The little girl scrunched up her face, looked at her mother, and after a few moments smiled. "Oh, Daddy, Sylvia and I are hungry. Make us breakfast, *please*."

"Daddy," Sue continued, looking down at her apparently junior marital partner, "You heard the magic word. See you later." She rolled over as I, resignedly, arose from bed.

A half-hour later, the aroma of freshly brewed coffee wafted into the bedroom, finally awakening Sue. She found the rest of her family in the kitchen gathered around the island. Marcia was sipping orange juice as she waited for her oatmeal to cool. I was next to Sylvia, who was in a jumper seat attached to a chair. I was spooning jarred junior breakfast into her busy mouth and sipping coffee. Sue observed the scene. "Where's mine?"

"Marcia," I said, turning to her. "You heard your mother."

She looked puzzled for a moment, giggled, and turned to her sister. "Your turn, Sylvia."

We both broke up. When she finished laughing, Sue pointed a finger at me. "What are you doing, training another stand-up comic?"

"Just keeping up the family tradition."

"But, Daddy, I'm *sitting*."

After a few more laughs, I hugged my older daughter. "You sure are sweetheart."

Sue poured a cup of coffee and sat down next to Marcia. "What's Daddy making Mommy for breakfast?"

The little girl shrugged.

"How's pancakes?" I asked, pointing to a metal mixing

bowl partly filled with batter.

"A little fattening," Sue replied, sipping her coffee. "But good."

AFTER BREAKFAST, WE WENT TO A CHILDREN'S MUSEUM recommended by Marcia's kindergarten teacher, followed by lunch out, and a playground. At home while the children were napping, Sue and I settled down in the living room with a bottle of pinot noir. As frequently happens when law partners get together for drinks, we talked shop.

Sue was expansive about her active and varied appellate practice. While her unit handled nearly all of the insurance defense appeals, she was able to farm out most of the mundane ones to her juniors and keep only the more difficult and interesting cases. Even better, she had many non-tort appeals, some with fascinating legal issues.

Though happy for her success, I envied the variety of cases that made up most of her case-load as opposed to my boring collection of insurance defense ones. While Alex and I were making fair progress on the Phillips encyclopedia, it was far from exciting. I was annoyed to realize that Ramos, with all of its frustrating problems, was one of my favorite cases. At least it had some interest and didn't put me to sleep, so when Sue finished her litany and asked about Ramos, I was pleased to bring her up to date. "You remember my telling you about the witness who said the old man paid for his dinner that night?"

She nodded. "You hoped that would show the plaintiff and all three witnesses had dinner together before the accident, and that the jury would know that the so-called accident was a setup. Anything new on that?"

"Unfortunately yes." I told her about the corrective affidavit. "So now he says he meant his father, and in a follow-up examination, he said it was his father's birthday gift that paid for it.

She nibbled a piece of sushi roll. "Did the investigator reach the father or sister?"

"*She* wouldn't talk to him, and the father's in a nursing home after a stroke."

Sue topped up our glasses. "I wouldn't do any more on that. No one will believe that bull."

I shook my head. "Almost no one."

"Dear Judge Robbins."

I nodded. "Still, I agree with you. There's nothing more I can do about it. There *is* something else pending." I told her about Ralph Lawrence Santo.

"That sounds great," she chirped. "The parole officer could kill the plaintiff's case."

"Big if," I replied. "The guy's out on extended sick leave."

"Anything new on doing capital defense cases?"

"Yeah. I got a response from the *Death Penalty Infor-*

mation Center. They told me there are three organizations doing that work. One is an *ABA* project. I need to do some research on them."

Her mouth tightened. "Well, if you're serious, get off your ass and do it."

I let out a breath. "You're right. I'll do it as soon as I can, but currently I'm doing the boring work to make my queen and two princesses richer. . . . It's really a job I should assign to Alex."

She nodded. "I'll remind you."

CHAPTER
FORTY-ONE

THREE MONTHS AFTER THE CASE was restored to the trial calendar, it reached trial. I made my application for disclosure and discovery adjournment provided in the order, and as I'd anticipated, Judge Robbins was far from generous. While the order gave me at least six months, Robbins grudgingly gave me two months in one month segments. The judge's position was that investigation based upon witnessess's testimony at deposition was too imprecise to warrant further adjournments. He wanted to know exactly what would be found before he granted time to search for it.

I was afraid to disclose my search for proof of Raymondo's New Mexico conviction under a different name. I'd spoken to Mark Stevens about the problem. He was a little annoyed that Charlie hadn't filled him immediately, but recognized that these things happen. Fortunately he had a contact in New Mexico he'd refer Charlie to. His instructions to me were to get what time I could, then try the case and not worry. Mark was a gem, and Jerry Arthur was lucky to have him.

THE TRIAL DATE LOOMED. While not happy with the disclosure and discovery I'd gotten, I realized it was time to bite the bullet. I assumed we'd be sent out to select a jury, but Judge Robbins called us into his robing room for a conference. When we were seated, he leaned his chin on his cupped fingers, pointed his index finger, and stared into my eyes. "Your moment of truth has arrived, Andrews."

"Oh?" I replied, returning the judge's stare, and straining to hide my amusement.

"This is your last chance to settle the case within policy limits." He turned to face Ayala. "I assume you're still willing to give him a small discount."

The man gave the judge a smile. "I think I can persuade my client to give a tiny one, Your Honor."

"Very reasonable Mr.—" the judge looked down at the file. ". . . Ayala." He turned back to me. "You're still in luck, Andrews. How much do you need?"

I shook my head. "Three million, and I think I can persuade the company to waive the costs and disbursements they could get against the plaintiff."

The judge's stare slowly evolved into a glare. "I'm getting sick and tired of being subjected to your tasteless jokes."

I felt like slugging the man but restrained myself. "Then why don't you recuse yourself, so that a different judge can be stuck hearing them?"

Robbins' face reddened. Then his expression changed to a smile. "No, Mr. Andrews, as much as I'd love to be rid of you, I need to be on this case so that this poor plaintiff will get a fair trial."

"And my defendant will be railroaded," I added.

"Then get out of here and go to—" Robbins consulted a chart taped on his desk— "room 313, and select your jury." We were about to rise when Robbins continued, "And don't let me hear that you're playing games with the jurors."

"I'll do what I need to protect my client," I replied, trying to keep my newly learned anger out of my voice.

"Then get ready to spend some time in the civil jail." Robbins pointed to the door.

As we were about to leave, I asked, "Excuse me, Your Honor, but how many alternate jurors shall we select?"

"Just pick the six regular jurors," the judge replied with a near devilish smile. "With an open-and-shut case like this one, alternates are a waste of time, and you don't need the extra peremptory challenge. . . . And by the way, Andrews, take your frivolous juror challenges to Mrs. Chan. She'll make all juror rulings."

OUR GROUP MADE ITS WAY to the jury section part, a suite of rooms divided into three sections. The largest compartment was the jury assembly room, where people summoned for jury duty waited until they were called for a case. There was a small waiting room as well and four jury selection rooms. Since Robbins had delayed in sending them out, We had to wait until after the lunch break. At 2:00 in the afternoon, room 32 became available, and we and our clients entered what appeared to be a miniature court room. Near the door were four rows of benches. The rest of the room was taken up by a jury box and three tables, one with a hopper for the clerk, and one each for the plaintiff and the defendant. A few minutes later the clerk, a dark-haired man in his forties with a neatly trimmed beard, led a group of thirty people into the room and had them take seats. He filled the hopper with slips of paper, turned the crank, removed a slip, and read out a name. A woman answered and was told to take the first seat in the jury box. He repeated the operation five times. The box contained four men and two women. He slid the slips of paper into slots on a board, handed the board to Ayala, and nodded.

Ayala read the juror information on the slips, rose, faced

the jury box, and said, loud enough to be heard by all the prospective jurors in the room, "My name is Miguel Ayala. I am the attorney for the plaintiff. That gentleman—" He pointed to Ramos, who was seated in a wheel chair—is Juan Ramos. He is the plaintiff in this case. He was injured in an auto accident caused by the extreme negligence of the defendant."

I had already risen. "Mr. Ayala, you know that is highly improper. What you said is only your claim, and that the defendant contends that the so-called accident was intentionally caused by your client's driver, so please stop trying to prejudice these prospective jurors."

"I guess so," Ayala replied as I seated myself. "In any event, do any of you folks know, or have any of you met, either me or Mr. Ramos?"

All the people in the jury box shook their heads.

Ayala turned to the ones seated on the benches. "That question was for everyone. Do any of you know, or have any of you met, me or Mr. Ramos? If you have, please speak up."

No one did and Ayala turned to me. I rose and stood in front of the jury box. "Ladies and gentlemen, my name is William Andrews, but I'm known as Bill. This gentleman—" I pointed at Alex—"is Alexander Tietel. We are lawyers with the firm of Franklin, Powers and Rush. And this gentleman," I pointed to Joel, who was dressed casually.

I had instructed him not to wear a suit, but to look like the working stiff he was—"is Joel Berger. He is the defendant. Do any of you know or have any of you met, Joel, Alex, me, or anyone from my firm?"

A man in the last row spoke up. "My sister's a secretary with your firm."

"What is your name, sir?"

"Julius Harris."

I turned to Ayala, who nodded. "Thank you for your honesty, Mr. Harris. You are excused from this case."

When the man had left, Ayala rose again, facing the woman in the first seat. "Ms. James, do you or any member of your family have any interest in an insurance company that insures against claims or liability for accidents involving personal injury or property damage?"

She looked at him strangely, but said no.

He asked the same question of the other five and got the same answer.

I knew that, while the question was proper, Ayala's purpose was not, and that I had to cover myself. I rose. "Ladies and gentlemen, Mr. Ayala's questions about insurance may be confusing to you." I held up a sheaf of papers and pointed to the top one. "This is the complaint in this case. It shows that Juan Ramos is the plaintiff and Joel Berger is the defendant. I assure you that they are the only parties to this case."

Ayala was already shouting, "You can't say that. You can't tell them there's no insurance."

"I didn't say that."

"Yes, you did, and it's a lie. There is insurance, and you're the insurance company's lawyer."

I glared at the man and pointed to the door. "Let's go see the judge."

FIFTEEN MINUTES LATER, we were in Judge Robbins' chambers, and Thelma Chan was seated at the head of the table. "What happened?" she asked.

"He told the jury there was no insurance," Ayala nearly shouted, pointing, "and I corrected him."

I was shaking my head. "Not so, Ms. Chan, and *I* asked for this meeting, so please hear me out."

She nodded.

"Mr. Ayala separately asked each of the six prospective jurors," I looked down at a yellow legal pad and quoted Ayala's question.

"A proper question, although six times is quite heavy-handed," she said.

"I agree, but I had to try to protect my client," I said.

She nodded. "How?"

I again looked down on the pad, and quoted exactly what I'd said.

"Perfectly proper," Chan said with a shrug.

"Then Mr. Ayala accused me of telling them there was no insurance, and when I denied it, he said I was lying, and that I was the lawyer for the insurance company."

The law secretary knitted her brow and looked at Ayala. "Is that what was said in front of the prospective jurors?"

"Yes," said Ayala, "so you see I had to protect my client."

She shook her head slowly. "Mr. Ayala, you have just spoiled an entire panel of proposed jurors. You obviously don't understand the rules concerning insurance. You are permitted to ask whether they have any interest in an insurance company, because the law says they are presumed to be prejudiced against plaintiffs, which gives you a challenge for cause. You, like many plaintiff's lawyers, used the question for the improper purpose of telling them that the defendant has insurance. Since Mr. Andrews, even if it's true, is not allowed to tell them there is no insurance, he can tell them that the only parties to the law suit are the plaintiff and the defendant. Frankly, I don't know whether this gets their minds off insurance, but it is an acceptable statement. Now let me set some rules for the rest of jury selection. You may not tell prospective jurors there is insurance, and Mr. Andrews my not tell them there isn't any. You are limited to asking the insurance question once to the entire panel, and Mr. Andrews may make his statement once to them. Do you understand?"

Both of us nodded.

"Good. Now go back to the jury part and select six jurors. I'll call the clerk and get you a fresh panel. *Don't* spoil them."

AFTER WE RETURNED TO THE SELECTION ROOM, the clerk brought in another group of thirty prospective jurors, and we started over. Ayala followed the rules, so that the process started more smoothly, and he got through his first round of questions without incident.

Then it was my turn. I questioned each of the six about their employment, and about their experience with and attitudes about litigation. Then I got to the specifics of the case. Turning to the juror in the first seat, an elderly, African-American man, I asked: "Mr. Hurley, during the trial of this case, you will learn that the front of the car being operated by Mr. Berger, and the rear of the car in which Mr. Ramos was a passenger, came into contact. I'm sure you will also hear testimony that Mr. Berger's car hit the other car in the rear, and Mr. Berger will tell you that the other car forcefully backed into the front of his car. What I need to know is whether you can keep an open mind, until you hear all the evidence, as to who hit whom, or whether the buzz words 'hit in the rear' prejudices your thinking so that you start the trial with the idea that the accident happened in a particular way."

At this point Ayala shouted, "Objection. You're prejudicing this juror to buy your crazy theory of this case."

"I am not. I'm just trying to find out if this gentleman is starting with a belief caused by those buzz words," I replied.

"And calling them 'buzz words' is prejudicing him against my poor client."

I shook my head. "Nonsense—let's see the judge."

Ten minutes later, we were again seated in the conference room with Thelma Chan again at the head of the table. She shook her head slowly. "Back so soon? Can't you children play nice? What happened this time?"

"He's prejudicing the panel," said Ayala.

"How?" she asked.

"By telling them that 'hit in the rear' are buzz words."

"They are," I replied. "And he told them that my telling them that defendant's position that the plaintiff's car hit defendant's car is prejudicing them with my 'crazy theory of this case'."

"Well, it *is* a crazy theory," said Ayala. "Accidents don't happen that way."

I pursed my lips. "This one did."

Thelma Chan turned and gave Ayala a questioning look. "Counselor, I'm having difficulty seeing where you're coming from. Are you saying that cars can't back up and hit another car? I know my car has a reverse."

"So does mine," I added.

"I didn't mean that," Ayala replied realizing he was painting himself into a corner. "But this was a high-speed traffic accident. Why would my client's nephew back into another car to cause an accident?"

"To get money from an insurance company. That's what Mr. Sanchez is trying to do."

Chan held up her palm. "Gentlemen, please! Save those arguments for your summations." She turned to Ayala. "Counselor, what Mr. Andrews is trying to do is to get jurors to start the case with open minds. Calling 'hit in the rear' 'buzz words' is a good description. It can create an assumption that the driver whose front bumper is in contact with the other car's rear bumper is always in the wrong. He's entitled to learn whether the prospective juror is starting with that assumption or has an open mind. The question of who hit whom is what your jury must decide, and the contention that plaintiff's car backed into the defendant's, while less usual, is not a crazy theory. Now, go back and see if you can finish picking a jury by yourselves."

The admonition was apparently successful, and by the end of the day, we had selected six jurors of mixed ethnicity, and hopefully with open minds. When we got back to Judge Robbins' part we were told to return the next day ready to start the trial.

CHAPTER FORTY-TWO

I LEFT THE SUBWAY AT 161ST STREET in the Bronx on a crisp, clear morning, a half hour before the courthouse opened, so I treated myself to a second breakfast at a coffee shop around the corner. "Morning boss," said Alex as he slid onto a stool next to me at the counter.

"How'd you know I'd be here?"

"I could say I read your mind."

"But you actually remembered me telling you they have good coffee, and for that it's my treat."

The waitress came over and we both ordered coffee, me with a buttered bagel and Alex with a blueberry danish. "Anything mew with Charlie?" I asked.

"He called. Asked when Raymondo would be in

court."

"He say why?"

"He wouldn't say. Asked me to call him when I knew."

"Very interesting."

AT 9:00, WE LEFT THE COFFEE SHOP, crossed 161st, and climbed the long flights of steps to the courthouse. With our attorney secure passes, we were able to avoid going through the metal detectors. We took the elevator to the third floor and walked over to Part 32, where we found the door locked. The calendar in the bulletin board showed the case scheduled for trial.

Five minutes later Joel Berger arrived, again dressed casually. "Where is everybody?" he asked.

I shrugged. "They'll be here if they still want money."

Ten minutes later, the latch clicked and the clerk opened the courtroom door. She looked at me and asked, "Where is everybody?"

"That's just what my client asked me."

"The judge wants to talk to the lawyers before I bring down the jury."

"I guess we'll have to wait for Mr. Ayala."

She shrugged and went to her desk.

Ten minutes later the man arrived looking flustered. He was accompanied by the plaintiff seated in a wheelchair, being pushed by his attendant.

"The judge wants to see us," I told him.

Ayala let out a breath.

"*Now*," the clerk added from her desk. She spoke into the intercom and signaled us to the robing room.

Robbins was all smiles as we entered and motioned us to seats. "Justice is about to triumph," he announced, looking into my eyes.

"I certainly hope so."

The judge shook his head. "I don't appreciate your gallows humor. I called you in here to give you a last chance to save your job."

Bored by the judge's continuous badgering, I kept my face impassive. "I certainly appreciate your kindness, Your Honor, but I'm a little confused about what you had in mind."

The judge shook his head. "I didn't think you were that dense, but I guess I'll have to lay it out to you. If you don't settle now, you're going to have to try the case, and the insurance company you work for will have to pay out at least the three-million-dollar policy, and maybe more. When that happens, you will most probably lose your job, and I'm trying to give you a last chance to keep from being fired. Have I made myself clear?"

I looked at the man, trying to keep contempt out of my expression. "Yes, Judge, you've made yourself clear, but you're laboring under a few misconceptions."

"Really?"

"In the first place, I'm not an employee of Capital Casualty. My firm has been retained by them to defend this lawsuit, which both they and I believe to be phony and dishonest. I have no authority from the company to make any offer of settlement."

"That's *nonsense*," Robbins nearly shouted, looking down at the file jacket. "They made a million-dollar offer, which this man—" he pointed at Ayala—correctly turned down as being much too low."

"That offer was made by Your Honor, not by Capital. There has never been any money on the table."

The judge let out an exasperated breath. "I've tried to help you, but you can't help someone who's not smart enough to accept it. Go lose your case." He pointed to the door.

"Judge," said Ayala. "I have a bit of a problem contacting my three witnesses to the accident. They haven't shown up yet."

Robbins shrugged. "Your plaintiff is here?"

Ayala nodded.

"Make your opening statements, and put him on. Then we'll see."

A few minutes after we returned to the courtroom, the six jurors were brought down by the court officer and seated themselves in the jury box. They appeared to be a good ethnic mixture. One man, and one woman, were African American. There were an Asian woman, a Hispanic woman, and two Caucasians, one male and one female as well. The judge greeted them and told them they would first hear the liability portion of the case, and "when you decide that the defendant is liable for the accident, you will then hear the evidence of this man's injuries." He pointed at the plaintiff.

I rose from my seat. "I object to Your Honor's language. The damage portion of the case may only happen *if* this jury is satisfied with liability. Your use of the term *when*, at this stage of the case, is an attempt to influence this jury in favor of the plaintiff, and is most prejudicial."

"Overruled," the judge snapped, frowning. "I'm doing no such thing. They mean the same thing. Now stop interrupting me."

"Exception," I replied.

The judge then explained that they would be hearing opening statements in which each lawyer would tell them what he intended to prove, but that the statements were not proof, and that the case had to be proved by evidence. He then turned to Ayala and told him to make his statement.

As Ayala rose to do so, Alex nudged me and pointed to Charlie DiNapoli in jacket and tie, who had entered the courtroom and seated himself. Ayala, who hadn't noticed him, placed several sheets from a yellow legal pad on the

podium and turned to the judge. "Thank you, Your Honor."
He then faced the jury and began. "Ladies and gentlemen,
as you know, I am Miguel Ayala, the attorney for Juan
Ramos, who was seriously injured in an accident. He was
a front seat passenger in a car driven by his nephew, Raymondo Sanchez. The car was stopped for a light, when a
car operated by this man—" he pointed at Joel Berger—
"drove at high speed into the rear of the car in which Mr.
Ramos was a passenger. Mr. Berger will claim that the
Sanchez car backed into him, but that's plain nonsense. You
will hear the testimony of three honest witnesses who will
tell you how the accident happened."

I was watching the judge carefully, and rose. "I object
to Your Honor nodding your head and indicating to the
jury that you believe that Mr. Ayala's version of the accident
is correct, and I respectfully request that you recuse yourself,
because you are obviously prejudiced against my client."

The judge's face reddened. "How *dare* you?" he
shouted. "I am doing no such thing. You are in contempt
of this court, and I will punish you for it after this trial is
concluded. Motion denied."

Ayala's opening statement continued and concluded
without further incident, after which I was called on to give
mine.

Before beginning, I told Alex to watch the judge carefully and to signal me if there was any non-verbal commu-

nication with the jury. I reintroduced myself and my client to the jury and began, "Ladies and gentlemen, Mr. Ayala wants you to believe that Mr. Berger drove his car into the rear of the car in which Mr. Ramos was a passenger, and that our position that the Ramos car intentionally backed into the Berger car couldn't have happened. I'm sure by the time this trial is over, you will find that this was a staged accident with imported witnesses, done for the purpose of stealing money." At that moment Alex tapped my arm and whispered into my ear. Facing the judge I said, "Your Honor, I object to your shaking of your head to show your disbelief, and I renew my motion for you to recuse yourself."

Robbins's face reddened. "Overruled and denied. I did no such thing. This further contempt will add to your punishment, and if you keep it up, your assistant can try this case while you spend your time in civil jail."

"Exception," I replied. I then made the balance of my opening statement without further problem, and, since the three witness had not yet arrived, the judge told Ayala to call the plaintiff.

"He speaks only Spanish, Your Honor."

"You should have told me earlier." Robbins turned to the clerk. "Kathy, order up a Spanish interpreter. . . . Find out how long it will take, and in the mean time send the jury to their room."

By 12:30, the interpreter had not arrived. The judge adjourned the trial until two-thirty, and we went out to lunch. I invited Charlie to join us, but when he learned that Raymundo wouldn't be here until the next day, he left saying he'd be back tomorrow with company. He wouldn't tell me more. I guess it was his revenge for my talk with Mark Stevens. Ayala was glued to his cell phone, desperately trying to locate his missing three witnesses.

At 2:45, the case was called to order. The judge announced that an interpreter would be available by three-thirty. He then asked, "Mr. Ayala, what's the status of your witnesses?"

The man smiled. "I was able to reach them, Your Honor. They thought the trial was tomorrow, and they'll be here in the morning."

"Okay, when the interpreter gets here, we'll hear the plaintiff and then adjourn until tomorrow." He turned to me. "That will give you and your insurance company some time to come to your senses."

"Thank you, Your Honor."

When the Spanish interpreter, a dark-haired, overweight woman arrived, the jury was called down, and the interpreter and plaintiff were sworn in. Ayala kept his client's testimony short. He limited it to testifying that his nephew, Raymondo, had taken him out of the nursing home and driven him to a Spanish restaurant for dinner. On the way back there had been a crash. He'd been knocked from the front seat and hurt badly. He didn't know how the accident had happened.

As I got ready to cross-examine, I wondered how well Ayala had prepared him. Could I make the man slip up as he'd done in his examination before trial? I decided I'd have to take a shot at it.

"Mr. Ramos, how long have you lived at the nursing home?"

"A long time."

I looked at my legal pad. "Would that be about seven years?"

"Yes, right after Carmen died."

"That was your wife?"

He nodded.

"Please answer in words."

"Carmen was my wife."

"Did you get many visitors?"

"Only Raymondo."

"He's your nephew?"

The man nodded, then caught himself. "Yeah."

"Before the accident, how often had Raymondo visited you?"

"About two times. He travels a lot."

"Who is Ruben Sanchez?"

"My nephew."

"He ever visit you at the nursing home?"

"No," Ramos replied, shaking his head.

"Is Carlos Perez related to you?"

"No, Raymondo told me he's a friend of Ruben."

"How's the food at the nursing home?"

"Not too good. I like Spanish food."

"Can you eat out from the nursing home?"

"If someone takes you."

"Before the day of the accident, had anyone ever taken you out to eat from the nursing home?"

"No."

"What was the name of the restaurant?"

"I don't remember."

"Did Raymondo buy you dinner there?"

"No, I paid for it all," he man replied shaking his head vigorously.

"It cost plenty?"

"Yeah." He nodded.

"Raymondo eats a lot?"

"He sure does. I bought him two full portions and he ate it all."

"How many portions did Carlos eat?"

At that point Ayala started to shout at his client in Spanish.

"Objection. Mr. Ayala is coaching the witness."

"Mr. Andrews is trying to trick my client. Carlos Perez

wasn't at the restaurant."

"Nonsense, I'm just trying to get at the truth. I'd like a translation of what Mr. Ayala said to the witness put in the record."

"No, that's not relevant," said the judge. "Let him answer the question."

"Neither Carlos nor Ruben were in the restaurant. I didn't buy them dinner."

"Exception," I said, knowing I'd have to fight it out in an appellate court.

"Ask your next question and stop delaying the case," said the judge.

I reached into my folder and pulled out a booklet. "Mr. Ramos, I show you the transcript of your examination before trial." He pointed. "Is this your signature where you swore it was true."

Ramos looked at the signature and nodded.

"Please answer with words."

"Yes."

"And during the examination I asked you some questions about the restaurant dinner you had before the accident and you testified that you ate *paella marinera*, and that your nephew, Raymondo ate two portions of *mariscada*. Do you remember testifying to that?"

"Yes."

"And was that true?"

The little man smiled broadly. "Of course, I only tell the truth."

"Good," I said, returning the smile. "I then asked you: 'What about Ruben and Carlos?'"

At that point Ayala started shouting objections that I was trying to trick the witness and that the answer to the question had been corrected by an affidavit. Robbins read the affidavit, sustained the objection without listening to me, and adjourned the trial to the next day.

WHEN THE JUDGE RETURNED TO HIS OFFICE, Thelma Chan burst in, shouting that the case would be overturned on appeal, and that they'd be back in civil court. At nearly the same moment, Ayala was on the phone with his mentor. "Carlos, that fucking judge is killing us with his kindness. If we win the case, we'll get murdered on appeal."

CHAPTER
FORTY-THREE

T HE NEXT MORNING BROKE BRIGHT AND CLEAR. Everyone, including Charlie, who was accompanied by two men in suits, but not Raymondo, was in court on time. Ayala told the judge that his key witness, the driver, had overslept but would be in court by noon. Before resuming the trial, the judge called the lawyers into his robing room, where he again read me the riot act about my need to settle the case, and got the same negative response from me. "Okay, Mr. Andrews," the judge said, pointing to the door, "go out and lose your case. Even I can't rescue a stubborn fool."

The jury was called down, and when they were seated, the judge announced: "Okay, Mr. Ayala, call your next witness."

"I call Mr. Ruben Sanchez."

As Sanchez walked to the witness box, I noticed that his co-witness remained seated. "Your Honor, Mr. Carlos Perez—" I pointed— "another plaintiff witness to the alleged accident, is still here. I respectfully move that he be directed to leave the court room while Mr. Sanchez is testifying."

The judge, facing the jury, screwed up his face. "Stop being so fussy, Mr. Andrews, they'll only tell the truth. Motion denied."

"Exception," I replied.

Ruben testified exactly as he had in his examination before trial. On cross I tried to bring up the pre-accident dinner with his uncle, which he denied claiming he had eaten at home. "Then why did your uncle say in his examination before trial that you and Carlos had eaten *paella* same as him?"

Ayala was on his feet objecting, and the judge sustained the objection.

Carlos Perez's testimony went the same way and the judge excoriated me in front of the jury for asking the same questions he had ruled against during Ruben's testimony. We adjourned for lunch with the expectation of having Raymondo testify in the afternoon.

When the defendant's entourage, including Charlie and the two visitors came back from a lunch all paid for by me, we found Raymondo conferring with Ayala in between bites of an oversized hero. When court was convened, Ayala announced: "As my final witness, I call Raymondo Sanchez, the driver of plaintiff's automobile."

Raymondo rose, wiped the balance of his meal on his sleeve, and seated himself in the witness box. His testimony about the accident was, as expected, identical with his examination before trial. Near the end of it, Ayala asked: "After the crash, did you have the opportunity to observe the other driver, Mr. Berger?"

"Yeah."

"What did you observe about him?"

"That he must have been roaring drunk, because he stank of booze."

With that, Ayala concluded his direct examination.

As I rose, I told Alex to keep his eyes on Ayala and tell him if the man started giving the witness signals. I positioned myself between Raymondo and the lawyer, and smiling at the man, began. "You must have been pretty close to Mr. Berger to smell him. How close?"

"I stuck my head into his car."

"What kind of liquor did you smell?"

"How the f—heck should I know?"

"Well, what kind of liquor did you pour on Mr. Berger, or force down his throat?"

"I didn't do no such thing," the man nearly shouted.

"Wasn't it what you did when you staged accidents in New Mexico?"

"Like *hell* I did." Raymondo's face reddened.

"But you did live in New Mexico. Didn't you?"

". . .I been there."

"For three years as an inmate of the New Mexico State Penitentiary in Santa Fe. Wasn't that for staging auto accidents?"

"No way."

I shook my head. "That's not what your parole officer, Paul Martini, told me." I turned toward the visitors section. "Mr. Martini, please stand up." A slim, dark-haired man, one of the two with Charlie, rose. "You know Mr. Martini. You skipped out on him, and he, and this state police officer, are here to arrest you and take you back to finish your sentence."

Raymondo sprang up and bolted for the exit, but was stopped and held by Charlie and his two guests.

"Oh, my God!" moaned Judge Robbins with a chagrined look, while Thelma Chan sat grinning.

THE END OF THE RAMOS TRIAL WAS ABRUPT. Raymondo was cuffed and taken away to await his extradition hearing, and the jury was sent to their room. The judge's change of attitude was also abrupt. He gave me a friendly smile, then turning to Ayala, frowned and demanded: "Does plaintiff rest?"

"I-I guess so. . . Your Honor," the poor man nearly stammered.

"I assume you are moving to dismiss at the end of plaintiff's case, Mr. Andrews?"

"Yes, Your Honor," I replied.

"Motion granted." The judge turned back to Ayala. "And I suggest you look for another occupation. I will be reporting your misconduct to the Office of Court Administration."

EPILOGUE

T HAT EVENING, SUE AND I HAD a leisurely dinner, and were sipping brandy laced coffee. "So, Ramos is finally behind you."

I nodded.

"Think it'll stay there?"

"Probably. I can't see Ayala appealing. He now knows he has a real loser. He'll be lucky if Attorney Ethics doesn't rap him hard on his knuckles for not learning it sooner." As much as I knew he brought the problem on himself, I felt sorry for the man. He too was a victim.

"I'm glad you won," Sue continued, "but I was looking forward to destroying Robbins on appeal, and maybe sending him back to the civil court where he belongs."

I shook my head. "I knew there was something I forgot to tell you. After the trial, I dropped in at Judge McKenna's chambers to fill him in. He had some interesting news."

"Oh?"

"His friend at the Appellate Division told him they're shipping Robbins back to the civil court for some basic training."

"What happened to his protection from Williams? He lose it?"

"No he still has it, but it seems Mrs. Robbins told her friend, Kathy Williams, that her stupid husband needed to be taught a lesson. McKenna thinks they'll keep him down there for six months to a year, and maybe he'll learn something."

A smile flickered on Sue's face, then faded. "That's great, but I feel sorry for his poor law secretary."

"Don't," I continued. "Williams just put her in line for the next civil court judgeship."

Sue's smile broadened. "Wonderful! She deserves it. . . . I assume Jerry Arthur is pleased with the result in Ramos."

"Ecstatic."

"But what about you?"

I smiled wanly. "I have to be glad I won."

"But?"

"But now all I have is the boring stuff," I groaned.

"It'll pay the girls' college and graduate school tuition."

"There's that," I replied without enthusiasm.

"You do have some plaintiff's trials coming up."

I poured refills, took a sip, then shrugged. "The other side of the coin, though a little more exciting."

"What about the post conviction death penalty cases you've mentioned?"

"I've been looking into it, but it's a double edged sword."

"How so?" she asked, scrunching up her brow.

I took another sip of coffee wondering how to tell her. Sue's working class background, gave her occasional money worries about the prospective high cost of the girl's private school, college and graduate school education, despite the amount I've socked away from my tennis career. "You re-member what I told you about my correspondence with *Death Penalty Information Center*?"

She nodded. "I assume they got back to you."

"Almost immediately. They pointed me to a lot of in-ternet research that I had Alex do."

"And?"

"He found there's a three day continuing legal educa-tion course run by a capital defender group next month in Albany. If the plaintiff's trial starting next week ends soon enough, I'll have time for it."

"So what's the problem?" she replied showing more ap-proval than I'd expected.

Gordon's not in favor. He says we don't know what the inside of a criminal court looks like, and besides, we do too much *pro bono* as it is."

She compressed her lips. "I think he's right, but you've got to learn more about it, and your mental health *does* count."

www.ingramcontent.com/pod-product-compliance
Lightning Source LLC
Chambersburg PA
CBHW030528030726
47495CB00004B/897